Entrance to
the Tunnel

Turn
Two

The Track

The
Infield

Turn
One

Garages

Pit Road

Start / Finish Line

The
Grandstands

Revver's
Tree

Loudspeakers

REVVER

THE SPEEDWAY SQUIRREL

REVVER
THE SPEEDWAY SQUIRREL

Sherri Duskey Rinker

ILLUSTRATED BY **Alex Willan**

BLOOMSBURY
CHILDREN'S BOOKS
NEW YORK   LONDON   OXFORD   NEW DELHI   SYDNEY

BLOOMSBURY CHILDREN'S BOOKS
Bloomsbury Publishing Inc., part of Bloomsbury Publishing Plc
1385 Broadway, New York, NY 10018

BLOOMSBURY, BLOOMSBURY CHILDREN'S BOOKS, and the Diana logo
are trademarks of Bloomsbury Publishing Plc

First published in the United States of America in September 2020
by Bloomsbury Children's Books

Bloomsbury books may be purchased for business or promotional use.
For information on bulk purchases please contact Macmillan Corporate
and Premium Sales Department at specialmarkets@macmillan.com

Library of Congress Cataloging-in-Publication Data
Names: Rinker, Sherri Duskey, author. | Willan, Alex, illustrator.
Title: Revver the speedway squirrel / by Sherri Duskey Rinker ; illustrated by Alex Willan.
Description: New York : Bloomsbury Children's Books, 2020.
Summary: Revver the squirrel dreams of being a race car driver—or at least a member of
the pit crew—but his squirrel survival lessons have taught him nothing about engines.
Identifiers: LCCN 2020007343 (print) | LCCN 2020007344 (e-book)
ISBN 978-1-5476-0361-9 (hardcover) • ISBN 978-1-5476-0362-6 (e-book)
Subjects: CYAC: Squirrels—Fiction. | Automobile racing—Fiction. | Pit crews—Fiction.
Classification: LCC PZ7.R476 Rev 2020 (print) | LCC PZ7.R476 (e-book) | DDC [Fic]—dc23
LC record available at https://lccn.loc.gov/2020007343

Book design by Jeanette Levy
Typeset by Westchester Publishing Services
Printed and bound in the U.S.A. by Berryville Graphics Inc., Berryville, Virginia
2 4 6 8 10 9 7 5 3 1

To find out more about our authors and books visit
www.bloomsbury.com and sign up for our newsletters.

For William "Bill" Campana
For Chris Buescher —S. D. R.

For Harley, who loves squirrels —A. W.

1

In a grove of tall trees, the sunlight sparkled through branches and a light breeze wiggled new leaves. It was late spring. Finally, the first warm winds of the year made everything feel hopeful and happy.

Through the spots of light, four giggling young squirrels lined up, ready and waiting. Their course was decided: jump off the low branch, run around the trunk, head straight to the maple tree, go down the hill, and then climb back up here.

"Is everyone ready?" asked Bounce, hopping up and down.

"Vr-vr-vr-VRRROOOOM!" roared another one.

"Ready!" the other two said, excited.

"Okay, then! Ready, set . . ."

"NOOO!" yelled Revver before his brother could finish.

"Not again!" Revver's siblings moaned. Revver stomped in front of Bounce and put his nose against his brother's. "You're *supposed* to say, 'Drivers! Start your engines!'" Revver was SO annoyed. *How many times do we have to go through this? Everyone knows THIS is how to start a race!*

"Well, *first*," Bounce argued, "we're *not* drivers.

And second, we don't *have* engines. *And third, you don't even know what an engine IS!*"

"Oh, *brother.* Here we go again," their tiny sister, Sprite, whispered under her breath.

"I KNOW what an engine is," Revver insisted.

"What, then? What IS it, then, *huh?*" Bounce demanded.

"That's easy," Revver said. He had watched *millions* of races from their nest overlooking the racetrack. He knew *exactly* what an engine was! "It's the loud, smelly *rumbly-ma-jingy thingy* with all the twisty pieces underneath the lid."

"The *rumbly-ma-jingy thingy?!*" Bounce was losing his patience.

"Yes. And I don't really know what it does *exactly*, but it is *very* loud, and I know that it's *very* important."

"So you don't *really* know . . ."

"Of course I know. I just told you."

"No, you just said you *don't* know. But I **know** FOR SURE that squirrels *don't* have—"

Sprite ran over to Bounce. She squeezed his

wrists to hold him still. She had to stand on her tippy-toes to look up at him. "Bounce, *please*, just say it the way he likes it," Sprite pleaded in a whisper. "It's important to him. Anyway, what difference does it make how we start? Let's just *race* already."

Bounce was going to argue when: RRRRRRRIIIIIPPPPP!

The sound was so startling that everyone stopped talking. Then an awful smell hit the air, and three squirrels cupped their front paws over their noses and groaned. The fourth squirrel, the oldest and biggest of them all, just grinned.

"Hmm," said Farty, patting his belly, "a loud and smelly *rumbly-ma-jingy thingy* . . . Guess what? I DO have an engine!"

It was quiet for a split second before all four of them fell onto the grass, laughing.

2

"Whatcha makin'?" Revver asked Sprite as he leapt up to her. She sat in a little hollow under their tree, twisting and braiding long blades of grass together.

"I'm not sure yet," she said. "I'll figure it out as I go along."

This was Sprite's talent. She took grass or thin stems or long weeds and turned them into things. Revver loved watching her paws flying around when she did this, moving and twisting *so fast*. In a matter of minutes, plain things turned into something else.

Often she made ropes and swings. She would hang them on the branches of the tree, where she could swing or spin from them or jump from one to another, right side up and upside down. Sprite was also an amazing acrobat.

Sometimes Sprite wove little bowls or baskets. Revver loved watching her pick simple, straight things from around the grove and turn them into other, beautiful shapes. It was like magic.

Recently she had started making chains that she wore around her neck or wrists. She gave Revver a thick, handsome chain made from orange reeds that he always wore around his ankle. She created chains for Bounce and Farty, too, but they always seemed to break or lose theirs.

Once, she had spent many days making a long, beautiful one for Mama to wear as a necklace. It was a very fancy design with lots of different-colored stems and a little acorn attached to it. Revver thought it was the most beautiful thing Sprite had ever made, and he told her so. He could tell she was proud.

But Mama didn't seem to care much for her present. "Oh m-my!" Mama stuttered as she held it, looking uncertain. "Um, hmm . . . Well, I'd be *very* afraid I would break this or get it caught on something. How about if I put it in this little hollow for safekeeping?" Mama then dropped it into the bottom of the burrow in the tree.

Sprite had nodded politely, but Revver just knew her feelings were hurt. She had worked so hard to make this special gift. He even thought he saw tears in Sprite's eyes, but he had never seen her cry before, so he wasn't exactly sure.

It just broke Revver's heart to think that his sister might be sad.

Whenever Sprite did her twisting and weaving, Revver would sit and watch for a while, and then he'd jump up and say, "Sprite, watch me! Watch how fast I am!" And he would run off toward *something* and back, as fast as he could.

"That was *really* fast, Revver. I'm *sure* that was faster than last time!" Sprite would always say.

"Do you think I was faster than Bounce?"

"I'm not sure. But you're *definitely* getting faster."

Revver was obsessed with *fast*. *Fast* was Revver's favorite thing.

Bounce was always faster than Revver. It never mattered to Bounce, but it *really* bothered Revver. Sprite and Farty were always third and fourth or fourth and third. Neither one of them ever cared.

"Just *run for fun*, Revver!" Sprite would tell him. But Revver was totally fixated on going *faster*. "I want to be the fastest! I want to WIN," Revver would say, and Sprite would sigh and roll her eyes. She knew where he got these ideas: he was ALWAYS watching that loud, smelly track below the nest. Like Mama, Sprite did not like this one bit. *Cars are dangerous!* Everyone knew that. Everyone except Revver, of course.

3

The next day, while Sprite sat weaving, Revver ran back and forth as usual. But each time he returned, he dragged a new item. Soon, he had a great pile of things from around the grove: sticks, black walnuts, big chunks of bark, and some stems.

"And what are YOU doing?" Sprite asked, barely looking up from her project.

"I wanted to make something, too! So I'm going to make a car."

"A *car*?!" Now Sprite looked up. "What are you going to do with a car?!"

"I'm going to get in it and go FAST!"

"Oh, brother." Sprite sighed. "Do you really

know how to make a car?" Sprite looked at his pile. She doubted this plan.

"Of course."

"Well, will you know how to make it STOP?" Sprite already knew the answer. Revver was not good at thinking things through.

Revver thought about this awhile. He didn't really care about STOPPING. He mostly cared about GOING. But she had a point. He should consider this. Really, he *should*.

But Revver had no time or patience for considering. Instead, Revver said exactly what Sprite assumed he would say. "I'm not sure yet. I'll figure it out as I go along."

Sprite shook her head and whispered, "Oh, *brother*."

Revver went right to work. He had no trouble fitting pieces together. Since the day he could first peek out over the nest, he had studied the track and racing. He knew *exactly* how a car should look!

He made a box out of bark chunks and stuck

the pieces together with sticky tree sap. He made a place where he, the driver, would sit. He picked four black walnuts, the roundest he could find, and tied them to the bottom of his project with thick stems.

"What are those?" Sprite asked when she looked up.

"These are the *go-a-rounds*," he said confidently. Sprite shrugged.

Then Revver put a lid on the front part of the box.

He knew that he needed something special under the lid. Of course, his car needed a *rumbly-ma-jingy thingy*. Something loud. And lots of twisty things.

He grabbed some small, twisted branches, threw them in, and arranged them a bit. There. That looked right. Now for the noise. This would be harder.

Finally, he had an idea.

"Can I use this?" Revver asked Sprite, pointing to a little basket she had finished making.

"Sure," said Sprite, who was already working on something else.

Revver took the basket and quietly tiptoed over to a nearby flower, where a big, fat bee had just landed. With his paw, he trapped the bee inside the basket, ran to his car, dumped out the angry bee, and closed the lid. Just like he thought, the bee made a LOT of noise. *This sounds just about right!* He had started his engine! Revver was so excited!

He got into his car, took a deep breath, and closed his eyes. He was READY, ready to rumble through the grove at blazing speed!

He waited. And waited. And waited.

Nothing happened.

He thought through his plan, and it seemed like he had all the important parts: he was sitting inside, the *go-a-rounds* were ready, the *rumbly* was rumbling . . . *What's wrong?* He just could not imagine why his car was not *going*.

Sprite glanced up at Revver. He looked very serious and determined as he sat in his wood box on top of walnuts. She quickly turned her face so that Revver would not see her laughing.

At last, Revver got out of his car. As he opened the lid to free the bee, *zap!* The angry bee stung Revver's paw before it flew away.

He was stunned by how much it hurt! "Ouchie, ouchie, ouch, OUCH!" He jumped around, licking and rubbing his sore paw. A shock wave of pain went from his paw and up his arm. Revver shouted, "It gave me a z*ap!*"

"Technically, it was a *sting*."

"It hurts SO much!"

"You kind of deserved that," Sprite said, very matter-of-fact. Revver, still rubbing the bump on his paw, finally sat down next to his sister while she worked.

Sprite could tell Revver was upset. "You made a very nice car, Revver," she said.

"But it doesn't *go*," he said sadly, kicking a piece of dirt.

"Well, I still think it was very clever of you to build it."

He knew that his sister was trying to help, but he didn't feel better. *All this work for nothing*, he thought. He was never going to go very fast *this* way. He needed to figure out something else.

4

The idea came to him right after his mother, brothers, and sister left the nest to scamper around and find food. They always began their day doing all those "normal" squirrelly things. Revver never cared much for the normal things that other squirrels did.

Ever since yesterday, he couldn't stop thinking about the car he'd built. Well, the car he'd *tried* to build. Cars were supposed to *go*! And he'd had big hopes of going *so fast!* . . . and then *nothing*. Sprite tried to make him feel better about it. But he didn't feel better. Not. At. ALL.

He stared up at the top of their tree from the

nest. Lying on his back, he sighed. And then *it hit him*! It zoomed toward him in a blur. It moved SO FAST that he didn't have time to get out of the way. A *something* fell from the top of the tree and conked Revver on the chest. "YOUCH!" He jumped up as the mystery object bounced off him and landed in the bottom of the nest.

Revver rubbed his sore chest with his sore paw—which still hurt from the zap he'd gotten yesterday. He picked up the *something* that had hit him and examined it: a large chunk of broken branch that had fallen from the treetop. *Whoa— that happened so fast!*

And that was how the idea STRUCK him.

He leapt from the nest and climbed UP, higher and higher, as fast as he could. Finally, Revver reached the very tip-top of the tree. The ground was a long, LONG way down. He was SO excited! The sun was just peeking up, and a warm glow fell onto the racetrack below. Looking at the view, he sighed. "It's even more beautiful from up here," he said to no one in particular. He could see the entire track in all its glory.

But he wasn't up here to watch the track; it was way too early for that anyway. No cars were running yet.

Now, for the first time since he'd started climbing, Revver paused. He'd seen enough races to know that he had to have a little strategy about this. The best drivers—the winners—waited until just the right moment to take the lead. They patiently raced right behind the leader, lap after lap, and then ZOOM! In a blink, they'd pull out ahead and take the checkered flag. Revver loved that great mix of speed and surprise.

So he tried hard to think like a race-car driver, which was not easy, since he was a squirrel. Waiting and thinking were not easy for him, but he forced himself. He licked one paw and held it up in the air to check the weather. No wind. *Perfect!* The temperature felt just right. He looked all around and thought hard. No rain. No fog. Nothing to block his view. Again, *perfect!* He thought about what other thinking and checking he should do, but nothing came to mind. He shrugged and guessed he was ready.

He looked down through the branches and saw the empty nest about halfway to the ground, just as he'd imagined when he looked up at this branch. Now that he focused on it, the nest looked A LOT smaller than he'd expected from up here. But still, he had a clear sight of it, and that was all that mattered. The excitement welled up inside him.

This might be his best idea EVER! He imagined himself as a race-car driver pulling ahead at the perfect moment. *Just like a chunk of broken branch*, he thought. He took a deep breath and roared, **"Vr-vr-vr-VRRROOOOM!"** as he sprang off the limb, scrunched himself into a tight ball, and aimed to land a cannonball dive, waaay down, straight into the nest.

5

A pain shot through him from his tail. In a flash, *smack!* He had landed HARD on his back. Now he tried to catch his breath. He was so confused! He reached behind him to rub his aching bottom. Where was the feeling of the wind whipping around him? Where was the thrilling rush of plummeting through the leaves? Where was the excitement of going faster than he'd ever gone before in his entire life? *What happened?!*

His sister glared at him from over his head. She looked down at him. He looked up at her.

"REVVER!" she yelled so loudly it made him jolt. "What in the WORLD do you think you are doing?!" As she screamed into his face, spit flew into Revver's eyes.

Understanding slowly settled over him . . . The shooting pain in his tail. The rough bark digging into his back. Only sky above. Sprite had yanked him back to the branch by his tail at the *exact moment* he had gotten airborne! She was much stronger than she looked.

The NERVE of her! "You followed me up here?!"

"You're darn right I did! I just *knew* you were up to something! I could feel it!"

He had no idea she was behind him on the climb up, but Sprite had a gift for that. Like a graceful little bird, she almost floated through the branches.

"Sprite! I had THE. BEST. IDEA. EVER! Why'd you have to stop me?!"

"Why'd I stop you? **WHY'D I STOP YOU?!** Because you would have died! Did you *really* think that you'd just softly land—*plop!*—perfectly, right in the middle of the nest? You'd actually DESTROY it with a stunt like that! You'd be dead, and the rest of us would be homeless! Do you REALIZE how heavy you are?! Do you REALIZE how fast you'd be falling?"

Revver thought for a second: *FAST! Yes! That was the whole idea!* His sister had ruined everything. He was angry.

"Are you LISTENING to me, little brother?!" she yelled into his face again.

Sometimes she really, REALLY annoyed him. In his opinion, she took the "big sister" thing way too seriously. She was older **by exactly one second**, and she was less than half his size. But even he had to admit the possibility of destroying the nest and DYING had not occurred to him. He *would* be MUCH heavier than the wood chunk that had landed on his chest.

His mind played back all the high-speed car crashes he'd seen on the track: cars flipping, parts and pieces flying everywhere. Big crashes left the cars shattered, hardly looking like cars at all. He thought about how that could have happened to their nest. He thought about what could have

21

happened to HIM! Now he felt a little embarrassed that, once again, Sprite was the smarter one.

At the idea of his family being homeless, his anger melted away a little.

He thought about his sore paw and his sore chest. Now he also had a sore tail. He imagined how much *more* he'd be hurting if he'd crashed from the treetop.

"Are you going to tell Mama?"

"I SHOULD, you know."

Revver looked into his sister's eyes. Even though she had just RUINED his whole plan, Revver still loved her. And he knew she loved him. He knew that she was always trying to protect him, and he hated upsetting her—which, unfortunately, happened A LOT.

She exhaled. "No. I'm not going to tell. But NEVER AGAIN, Revver. NEVER. AGAIN. I'm serious. Now, WHY? Why would you get such a **nutty** idea?"

"I wanted to go **REALLY FAST!**"

"Oh, *brother*," she said, annoyed. She helped him up and put her paws around his wrists and looked straight into his eyes. Then she said sincerely, trying to convince him for the millionth time, "Revver, squirrels—and YOU—**ARE** fast."

"Not *really* fast," he said sadly.

"Well, you're fast . . . ENOUGH."

Revver was about to argue, but then he stopped. There was no point explaining. No one ever understood, not even Sprite.

6

"Now, let's review the Essential Squirrel Skills," Mama announced.

All four children were crowded into the nest for Squirrel School. All of them were listening carefully. All except one. Revver's eyes were glued to the racetrack. A VERY exciting race was happening!

Revver did not like Squirrel School, anyway. It was SO SLOW.

"Recite," commanded Mama. She looked very serious.

"Scurrying!" cried Bounce while he popped up and down.

"Yes, correct. Please do try to sit still, dear. You're shaking the nest."

"Storing!" squeaked Sprite. She held a nut high above her head in one paw. She twirled on one toe and put the nut right into the hole in the tree. Of course she knew the answer; she always did.

"Lovely!" said Mama, clapping.

"Eating!" said Farty, with a pile of nuts on his belly. As he spoke, a loud squeak emerged from his underside, and a horrible stink filled the air. Bounce and Sprite groaned and turned their noses toward fresh air.

Mama sighed.

Sprite sighed, too. *"Brothers,"* she said under her breath.

"That's correct, Farty," Mama said. "And what about nuts?"

"Always smell them to make sure they are eggable."

"Not 'eggable,' dear, 'edible,' " said Mama. "That

means safe to eat. You're doing very nicely on practicing your words."

"Mama, may we *pleeease* be dismissed? We've been sitting still for *such* a long time!" said Bounce, who was definitely *not* sitting still. They had been gathered for only about five minutes—but that felt like an entire day to Bounce. Revver looked up, grateful and hopeful for the request.

"Patience, please," said Mama. "Now, what if there's a storm?"

Revver sighed and went back to concentrating on the race.

"Tuck into a hole in the sturdiest tree!" bounced Bounce, still bouncing.

"A bear or fox or coyote?" asked Mama.

"Run up a tree!"

"Hawk?"

"Hide!"

"Last resort?" asked Mama.

"Scratch, bite, and fight!" they all said. All except one.

"What about running along power lines?"

"Be careful! You might get *slapped with a* **zap**!" At the word "zap," Revver rubbed his still-sore paw.

"Perfect," said Mama. "Now for the most important: Should you go near cars?"

"No!" cried Bounce, who, looking very serious, had finally stopped bouncing.

"Never!" squeaked Sprite, glancing sideways at Revver.

"Never EVER!" said Farty.

"Because cars are . . ."

"DANGEROUS!" they all chimed in unison. All except one.

"Correct!" said Mama. *"And if you get near that . . ."*

"You'll end up FLAT!"

Mama looked proudly at her children. All except one. Once again, one of them was not paying attention. Once again, his face was turned down toward that racetrack, staring at all those *dangerous* cars!

Mama sighed. Since the four squirrels were born almost six weeks ago, they had all been good students. Well, all except one. Three of them had studied carefully and worked hard to learn the Essential Skills. But Revver paid no attention to anything except the action on the track below the nest.

From the beginning, Revver had been different from any other baby Mama Squirrel had ever had, in all of her many litters. When Revver was very tiny, he had been fascinated with anything *fast*. Unlike his siblings, who were annoyed or even scared, Revver watched with total fascination and complete delight when bees and birds—or even a stray acorn falling from the higher branches—zoomed by his face. When he was fussy, he wouldn't stand for cuddling and gentle rocking. The only way Mama Squirrel found to calm him was by carrying him tightly in her arms and running with him as fast as she could, until she was panting and exhausted. When storms approached and lightning struck and the wind howled, Revver's siblings would tremble and huddle down tightly into the nest. But Revver lifted his head high, loving the noise and the feeling of the wind blowing back his ears and rushing through his whiskers.

And once he was big enough to see down out of the nest and notice the track below, Revver was obsessed with, of all things, *car racing*!

Mama Squirrel's family had lived in this grove for generations, long before the track was even built. Rumors and horrible stories about problems between squirrels and cars . . . well, those went back many, many years. Every once in a while, a squirrel would venture out too far toward the road and, *oh!* Mama Squirrel shuddered when she thought about it! That **never** ended well for the squirrel.

And then the track was built. Many trees were knocked down to make room for it, and then the cars came closer to the grove than ever before. That made the squirrels in the grove hate cars *even more*. Everyone agreed that the awful, loud, smelly track was trouble. But, over the years, more squirrel generations came who never had known life before the track. So they had all learned to simply ignore it.

Mama Squirrel had spent *many* seasons in this tree, overlooking the track, but none of her other children had paid any attention to it. They all just ignored it, the way she'd learned to do. For the life of her, Mama Squirrel could not understand Revver's fascination with that track and those cars! Mama, like the others, just **DID NOT UNDERSTAND.**

7

While his siblings learned about finding food and staying safe, Revver learned about cars. Instead of watching Mama's demonstrations, Revver watched every practice, every qualifying trial, and every race. The roar of the cars made him giddy. Watching the crews working—changing tires, fueling the car, and then sprinting out of the way so the car could screech back into the race—made him so excited that his insides buzzed.

Instead of listening to his mama's lessons, Revver hung on the track announcer's every word from the loudspeaker. He strained his ears to hear anything he could from the shouting fans in the bleachers. The smells of fuel and burning rubber, the heat off the track, the blur of colors and sounds and engines and cheering, all happening at lightning speed—it was incredible. Revver was OBSESSED. If a tiny, young squirrel could be in love, Revver was, for sure, *in love* with auto racing. It was all just so *FAST!*

Now, at that very moment, the excitement of the race below overtook him. Without warning, Revver inhaled deeply, opened his mouth wide, and yelled out, **"*Vr-vr-vr-VRRROOOOM!*"**

Startled, his three siblings jumped and squealed in unison, "Please. Stop. Doing. That!"

"Ugh. That is so un-NOY-run!" muttered Farty, with a mouthful of food, as another stink bomb snuck out from under his tail and filled the nest with putrid air.

"*Annoying!*" Sprite corrected. Now *she* was annoyed with both of them. "*Brothers!*" she grumbled again.

"Revver!" Mama hollered, and Revver jumped

and faced her. "Have you been paying attention?!" Mama demanded.

Revver quickly nodded, as best as a squirrel can nod.

She continued. "Okay, then, Revver, this question is for you: name an animal, any animal at all, that is dangerous."

Revver stared at his mother. This was a simple question, but his mind had been so filled with racing that it was now completely blank. He couldn't think of anything!

"This is NOT a hard question, Revver. Just name *any animal* that is a threat to us."

Still, Revver's mind was empty. *Think! Think!* he told himself as he began to panic.

Leaning toward him as if she were stretching, Sprite whispered as loudly as she could into Revver's ear without being heard by Mama, "Dog!"

"Dove!" Revver said proudly.

Sprite rolled her eyes. *"Brothers!"* she whispered again.

"Dove?!" Mama yelled. "Did you say 'dove'?!"

"Ummm . . . yes?" said Revver, much less confident.

"Wrong! A dove is a sweet little bird. It's not dangerous at all! Oh, Revver, where do you get these ideas?"

Revver looked at Sprite to apologize, shrugging. He felt a pang inside. He really hated disappointing Sprite. She rolled her eyes and sighed again.

"Okay, let's just try another one," Mama said. "This is very, VERY important: How do you know if water is safe to drink?"

"Ummm, would you please repeat the question?" Revver's mind was now very much focused on a terribly exciting three-car race for the lead.

Mama Squirrel sighed. The other three children quietly said, *"Uh-oh."*

"How do you know if water is safe to drink?" said Mama, MUCH more loudly.

Revver stared at Sprite. Sprite stared at Revver.

She concentrated hard, trying to send him the answer through her mind.

It didn't work.

"Hmm . . . I'm sorry, Mama. I don't remember." He tried to face his mother, but his eyes wandered back over his shoulder—straining to see if all three cars had managed to make it through the turn side by side.

She sighed and shook her head. "REVVER! I've told you this before: Your obsession with that track! That SOUND you make! Those *dangerous* CARS! Nothing good can come of it! NOTHING!"

All the other children stared at Revver. They agreed with Mama! Revver snuck peeks at the track. He just couldn't stop himself.

This lecture was not new for Revver. He had heard it so many times he could recite it by heart. He TRIED to be a good student. He didn't like disappointing Mama and his siblings (and especially Sprite), but racing was just so . . . *wonderful*. And even though he'd tried to explain SO MANY TIMES, no one understood.

"Now," Mama continued, "you are all close to being fifty days old. I simply cannot let you leave the nest unless you have learned the Essential Skills."

Sprite raised her hand. "Mama, what exactly happens if we *haven't* learned the Essential Skills? Do we have to stay in the nest for fifty more days?"

No one had ever asked this question before.

"No, of course not, dear. You cannot stay here. I will have more children later this year, and I'll need this nest for the new babies."

"So we go no matter what?!" asked Bounce, bouncing with excitement. He loved the thought of being free to jump and climb all day, without having to sit still during Squirrel School.

"Well," Mama said, "I would need to double-check at the next Teachers Meeting to be sure, but I seem to remember that . . . yes, I believe . . . if you don't learn the Essential Squirrel Skills. . . . I might have to eat you."

Four small squirrels gasped in unison. No one moved or blinked. Even Bounce was still. Even Revver was paying attention now!

"D-d-did you say *eat* us?!" stuttered Farty, who, for once, had stopped eating.

"No, I said it's a *possibility*," Mama said in her matter-of-fact way. "Again, I would need to consult with the elder squirrel teachers to be sure, but I believe that's just the way it's always been done. OF COURSE, I can't send you into the wilderness if you can't care for yourselves. You wouldn't survive! What kind of mother would do that?"

"But, but . . . what kind of mother would *eat* us?!" cried Sprite.

Mama looked at their terrified little faces. "Oh! Don't *worry*, dears!" She tried to soothe them. "This is just how things are done in nature. But I've had *many*, MANY babies, and I have not had to eat *any* of them. Not a single one, ever! I'm sure it will all turn out fine!"

Then she looked at Revver and tilted her head. "At least I *hope* so."

All of Mama's babies stared at her with full attention. All except one. Revver was back to watching the race.

8

A race was starting. The humans had already taken their places in the stands, and Revver sat in the nest, ready and eager to watch. But he couldn't see clearly; everything looked so far away, and a thick fog covered his view. He was so frustrated that he couldn't see better! He couldn't understand how they could have a race in so much fog. It was dangerous! How could the drivers see? As he squinted to get a better view, the announcer suddenly called out through the loudspeaker, *"Drivers, EAT YOUR SQUIRREL!"*

Engines roared up, but Revver was startled. "Wait. That's not right," he said. Then he yelled,

"That's not it at all! It's *'Drivers, start your engines!'* You need to say it right!"

The announcer's voice boomed again. *"Drivers, EAT YOUR SQUIRREL!"*

Everything still looked so fuzzy and foggy that Revver felt dizzy. He was very frustrated by the fog and the strange announcement. He started yelling more loudly, "You need to stop the race. No one can see!"

"Drivers, EAT YOUR SQUIRREL!"

"Stop! That's not what you say! That's not right! That's NOT RIGHT! STOP SAYING THAT!"

"Stop saying what?" asked a sleepy Sprite, snuggled up at Revver's feet.

Revver jolted awake and sat up. He was breathing hard.

It was night. Everything was calm and quiet except for crickets chirping and a light wind rustling the leaves. His mother and his brothers were tucked into the nest with them, and Revver could hear them all breathing peacefully against his own panting.

"I just had an awful dream," Revver whispered.

Sprite nudged toward him. "You were yelling in your sleep. What was the dream?" she asked.

Still shaken, Revver recited every detail he could remember. Sprite patted his shoulder and rubbed his ears to calm him as she listened to every word. When Revver was finished, they were both quiet for a little while. Then Sprite held Revver's paw and looked her little brother squarely in the eyes. "Revver, I think I understand what that dream was trying to tell you. Do you think *you* understand what it means? Think about it, Revver. Do you think your dream might be telling you something—something *important*? Something that you need to do?"

Revver sat quietly for a minute. "Yes. I think I do. I'm pretty sure I know *exactly* what that dream was trying to tell me!"

This was the breakthrough Sprite had been hoping for! Mama's threat had gotten through to him! Finally, Revver would end his silly obsession with speed and the cars and the track and focus on mastering his Essential Squirrel Skills with the rest of them.

They settled in to go back to sleep. For the first time in as long as she could remember, Sprite could sleep soundly, without all the worry about Revver.

9

Sprite was still asleep when Revver dangled something in front of her face. "Look!" he said, excited.

She forced her eyes open and pushed herself up to focus. He held some kind of strange contraption and was waving it back and forth. As she looked more closely, she could see two acorn tops, joined together by a thick stem.

"What is it?" She rubbed her eyes with the backs of her paws, confused.

"Watch!" Revver said. He held the acorn tops, which were hollowed out, up to his eyes and looked through them.

"I still don't understand. What is it? What does it do?"

"I can see the track SO MUCH BETTER through these! I thought about what you said, about figuring out what the dream was trying to tell me, and I realized: I ALWAYS wish I could see the races better!" And, sure enough, Revver had made himself a perfect pair of tiny binoculars for watching the track. Now he would not miss a single, wonderful thing!

Sprite shot up. In a split second, she went from groggy to angry. "THAT'S what you think the dream was trying to tell you?!"

"Sure. What else could it be? It always bothered me SO MUCH that I couldn't get a better view from up here."

"Revver! OH MY WORD! The dream was trying to tell you that you needed to stop with all this racing and track nonsense and focus on Squirrel School! Because if you don't, Mama can't send you off on your own when you turn fifty days, and she might have to EAT YOU!"

"Don't be silly, Sprite. Mama isn't going to eat me." Revver was very calm.

"What makes you so sure, smarty-pants? Yesterday, she said, PLAIN. AS. DAY—"

"Sprite, when I watch the big humans coming and going from the track, they always say scary things to the little humans. They say things like, 'If you don't stop kicking your brother, we are turning around right now and going back to the car and going home!' or, 'If you don't quit that terrible whining right now, we're returning that nice new hat we just bought you.'

"But, Sprite, they *never* do it. It doesn't matter whether the little human stops or doesn't. It's just a threat. They're bluffing. Just like Mama: she's BLUFFING. Sure, OTHER THINGS, like foxes and hawks, might want to eat us, but Mama would NEVER *actually* eat me! Jeez! *And you always say I never learn anything important by watching the track . . .* "

"Revver, but . . . I mean, you . . . but . . . you need." And then she stopped. "Oh, *brother*," she said so quietly that only she could hear. She forced herself not to cry.

"Revver, we are NOT humans. We aren't the same."

"Please don't remind me," Revver said. Loving speed and cars would be so much more acceptable if he were not a squirrel. It would be so much easier to find someone who *understands*.

Revver had already put the acorns over his eyes to watch some cars driving onto the track. It was no use. Maybe Revver knew more than she did about big humans and little humans. But Sprite knew one thing for sure: Mama did not bluff.

10

The day started like most days. Revver, now with his new acorn binoculars firmly over his eyes, was totally absorbed in the track—the speeding cars, the sounds of engines and tires, the cheering of the crowd, the blare of the loudspeakers, the exciting BANG! of the occasional crash followed by the hold-your-breath GASP! of the crowd, the delicious smell of the car fumes.

When the announcer welcomed the humans and asked if they were ready for the race, Revver nodded frantically, as best as a squirrel can nod. As soon as he heard the horns trumpeting the national anthem, he sat, ready and eager with his paw over his heart, just like he had watched the humans do it. The announcer called out, "DRIVERS, START YOUR ENGINES!" Mama Squirrel and the other children covered their ears. Revver inhaled deeply and let out his own, **"Vr-vr-vr-VRRROOOOM!"** violently vibrating the nest and all the branches and leaves around it.

"Oh! That horrible sound!" Mama shook her head.

"PLEASE. STOP. DOING. THAT!" his siblings said, but Revver couldn't help it. He wasn't listening to them anyway. And he had a whole day of racing to watch.

"*Brothers!*" Sprite moaned under her breath.

As the day passed, Mama left the nest to collect food. Her children were all busy in the tree with the usual squirrel activities. All except one.

Bounce hopped happily from tree limb to tree limb below the nest. He was smooth and quick. Only the rustling leaves gave away his location. He sped from here to there like a brown blur through the tree.

Farty was settled into the comfy V of some limbs, enjoying a huge pile of nuts and berries.

49

And, like a tiny high-wire acrobat, Sprite stood, perfectly balanced on the tiniest of twigs, only to leap gracefully and swoop down to a row of swings she'd made that were hanging on nearby branches.

Revver had the nest to himself. With the binoculars still in his paws, he leaned his elbows atop the side of the nest to watch a very exciting race. There was a close run for first place. Three cars skidded and traded turns taking the lead. One would get ahead on the straightaway. Another would get by in the corner. A third car raced right behind, just inches from the cars in front of it, waiting for the chance to pass. One car would try to pass. Another car would block the way. Engines raced and tires smoked. Revver held his breath as the white flag waved. He knew what that meant: *one more lap to go!* He was so excited he could feel his heart beating!

Squeal! Boom! There was action in the far corner! It looked like one of the cars had skidded out of control, but it was too smoky for Revver to see what had happened. He could hear more squealing and gasping from the crowd. He saw the audience jump to their feet.

Revver's heart was pounding. "What's happening? Who has the lead? Is everyone okay?!" he yelled. Not knowing was more than he could stand. He popped up on the tippy tips of his back paws, s-t-r-e-t-c-h-i-n-g, trying to make himself a little longer, a wee bit taller, with his binoculars pressed tightly against his eyes. He leaned WAY OUT of the nest to get a better view. The excitement was too much!

"Vr-vr-vr-VRRROOOOM!" From deep in his chest, the sound of excitement burst out of him.

And before Revver understood what had happened, he had vibrated himself right out of the nest!

Now he sped, face-first,

        right

           toward

              the

                ground!

He was going SO FAST! It was AMAZING! The wind rushed through his whiskers and whistled past his ears. "*Woo-hooooooo!!!* This must be what racing feels like!" he squealed with pure joy at the speed. He loved it!

Then he caught a peek at the hard ground, coming closer and closer, faster and faster. Instantly, he remembered how Sprite had saved him from jumping off the top branch. He remembered his visions of *what could have happened* that day. He flashed back to all the cars he'd seen after high-speed crashes—mangled and ripped, with pieces scattered everywhere. A bee sting and a tail tug would be NOTHING compared to this! *Uh-oh!* he thought. *NOW I'll know what CRASHING feels like!*

Revver squeezed his eyes shut and braced himself for a very bad ending.

11

"Shave Rebber!" someone screamed through a mouthful of food.

"What?!"

"He said, SAVE REVVER!" he heard someone else answer.

"Oh, brother!"

Bounce, Sprite, and Farty jumped into action in the branches below Revver. None of them were big enough or strong enough to catch him. All they could do was try to slow him down, break his fall, and hope for the best. There was no time for anything else.

Suddenly a brown blur came bouncing up, speeding toward Revver, pushing him and pausing his fall for a moment. The blur shoved into his stomach HARD. Revver coughed and gasped. Now he was coming back down again, but more slowly.

"Your turn!" Revver heard.

Another, much smaller brown blur swung from a branch and pushed at him. Again, Revver stopped falling for a tiny moment. He started falling back down again, even more slowly.

And then a *very* big, very heavy, thick blur pushed into him, hard. And again, the first blur. And then the littler, second blur again.

Each time, Revver stopped falling for a split second, and then he continued down more slowly. Each hit was slowing his fall.

"Now ALL TOGETHER!"

Finally, Revver was knocked sideways, with three brown blurs bouncing and pushing at him with full force, all at once.

Revver came to rest on his back with a *boom!* in a thick tangle of leafy branches, just a few feet from the ground. His binoculars bounced off him as Bounce, Sprite, and Farty landed around him, all weary and panting. They had worked together, jumping and pushing at him, to save him from the fall.

"Revver! Are you COMPLETELY nuts?!" Bounce gulped for air.

Farty sniffed the air. "Nuts?" he asked. "*Where?!*" Somehow, through all of it, he was still chewing.

"Revver!" Sprite squealed. "You almost killed yourself!"

"And we all could have died trying to save you!"

Revver did not hear a word. He was filled with a kind of excitement he had never felt before. His heart was pounding. His paws were shaking. He jumped to his feet. "Did you SEE that?! Did you SEEEEE?! Did you notice how fast I was going?! SO fast! WOW! That was AMAZING!"

"Oh, BROTHER!!! Did you hit your head on the way down, because I'M SURE what you meant to say was, 'Thank you all for saving my life'!" Sprite boomed. She was NOT pleased.

"Don't worry, Sprite. It was an accident—I promise! I was just watching the race, and I leaned out a little too far, and . . . *Oh!* The race! I need to see what happened!"

Revver started searching around for his binoculars.

"Oh, Revver! How will you *ever* survive in the wilderness?!"

Not even bothering to look up, Revver said, "You know, I've been thinking about this. I'm not very interested in the wilderness. I've decided that I'm going to live at the track." Revver spoke matter-of-factly. But if Revver was being honest, he would have to admit that he *hadn't* been thinking about it. Revver did not really *plan* anything. This wonderful idea had occurred to him that very second, inspired by the incredible feeling of SPEED that still had him tingling.

His siblings were so shocked by the very *idea* that they froze in place with their mouths hanging open. Then they all started talking at once:

"Oh, *brother!* Are you kidding?!"

Bounce jumped up and began hopping wildly. "The TRACK?! You're a SQUIRREL! What can you possibly *do* there, around all those DANGEROUS CARS?!"

"Cars!" Farty gulped as he swallowed. Cars were a scary thought.

All together, his three siblings chanted, "If you get near THAT, you'll end up FLAT!"

"What WILL you do there? How will you survive without any Essential Skills? What EXACTLY is your plan, little brother?!" asked Sprite.

Ugh! He really hated when she called him that. Revver said nothing. He tried to hide the fact that he was getting very annoyed and just kept searching for his binoculars. Sprite knew darn well that he had no plan, ever.

"I *have* skills," Revver said simply.

"Watching cars and wanting everything *fast* and making that horrible sound are NOT valuable skills."

"They are valuable to *me*. And maybe they would be valuable to someone. Maybe I have *different* skills. Maybe I just need to find someone who *understands*." And somehow, Revver just knew, if that *someone* existed, the track would be the place to find them.

They all felt scared and worried. All except one.

"Aha! Here they are!" Revver untangled his binoculars from around a nearby twig, thankful they were not broken. "I have to get back to the race to see what happened!" he said as he hurried up toward the nest. "Oh yeah, and thanks for saving my life and everything . . . ," Revver's voice trailed off as he scurried away.

Sprite's stomach was in knots. She was pretty sure that, as much as she loved her brother, she would never, *could never*, understand him. Would Revver ever get the chance to leave the nest at all? Even if he *could* prove to Mama that he had mastered his skills, Sprite had already helped save Revver's life TWICE in the last two days. Skills? DID Revver have a single *useful* skill? Sprite knew him better than anyone, and even she doubted it.

Sprite feared that, one way or another, Revver was doomed.

12

Once again, Squirrel School dragged on and on. And *on*. Revver *really* tried to pay attention, but the excitement of the track that day was too magical to ignore. And now he imagined himself down there, around the cars and the speed: up close! It just HAD to happen. He HAD to live at the track! He only needed to try a little harder to pass Squirrel School . . .

But just when he would make up his mind to focus on Mama and his studies, **vroooom!** a car would roar along the straightaway at full speed, and Revver could not help but watch the action into the next turn.

Revver had already gotten three questions

wrong. Mama was growing more and more irritated and Sprite felt more and more desperate for her brother. The nest felt sad and serious. Finally, Mama changed the subject to try to lighten the mood.

"So! Have you all thought about where you might like to live when you turn fifty days?"

They started nodding excitedly, as best as squirrels can nod, and shouting out their answers. All except one.

"I like that walnut tree *waaay* over there! Its branches are *perfect* for my ropes and swings!"

"I've seen a grove of pines off to the east. It has LOTS of trees and LOTS of solid limbs for jumping!" cried Bounce. He was so excited that the whole nest bounced.

"I think I will go to that joke tree!"

"Farty, I think you mean OAK tree," corrected Mama.

"Yes, OAK, I mean."

"*Oh, brother,*" Sprite whispered.

"Oh, that all sounds perfectly lovely!" said

Mama Squirrel, clapping her paws, as best as a squirrel can clap.

Now, Revver WAS listening, but he did not dare answer. He knew his plan would not go over well with Mama. She definitely would not approve. And he already knew his siblings' opinions on the subject.

Just then, a darkness fell over the group. Mama and all four children quickly looked up. The shadow passed by just in time for Revver to see a huge black hawk circling the tree.

The hawk took aim and swooped in, heading straight for the nest! Branches broke and leaves showered down on the squirrels. In no time at all, the hungry hawk was upon them.

There was no time for hiding, or running, or camouflage. They would have to scratch, fight, and bite to protect themselves.

Furry paws flailed. Teeth grabbed and chomped.

Squirrel squeals were muffled by the hawk's screech. Revver could barely tell Sprite or Farty or

Bounce apart as they tumbled and kicked. They were no match for the enormous bird. It felt nothing!

Suddenly, all of Revver's feelings rumbled up inside him—his frustration about never being *understood*, the hurt of no one believing that he had any real or important skills, and his anger at this awful beast, trying to swoop in and hurt his family. An idea came quickly, like a sudden, powerful thunderstorm. Revver gathered up all the energy from all his feelings. He imagined starting up a giant engine inside himself and making it *roar* to life. And then he bellowed out, louder and longer than ever before,

"Vr-vr-vr-VRRROOOOO-OOOOOOOM!"

The sound was so enormous that the entire tree—maybe the entire *world*—began to shake. The giant bird shook, too. Its eyes opened to the size of big black walnuts. For a split second, it was paralyzed with confusion and fear. It stopped moving at all. Then it squawked in terror and flew high into the sky and far, far away.

13

For a long time, everyone sat in the nest, panting. No one spoke. Farty let out a little squeaker in relief, but no one even noticed.

All of them had a few bumps, bruises, and scratches. Here and there, they had lost a few tufts of fur in the battle. But no one was badly hurt.

Everyone stared at Revver.

Revver looked around at everyone.

Time stood still.

What had just happened? It started to sink in. Tiny Sprite was suddenly overcome with joy. She jumped up, ran toward Revver, and wrapped her little arms around her brother's neck. The force nearly knocked Revver onto his back.

He was startled. Little Sprite WAS a lot stronger than she looked.

"Revver! You saved us! You saved our lives! You saved us, little brother! That crazy, awful, *beautiful* sound *saved us all!*"

His brothers began to cheer, clap, "high-paw," and pat Revver on the back while Mama nodded—as best as squirrels can nod. Mama went over and rubbed Revver behind his ears. She quickly wiped a tear from the corner of her eye, trying to hide her own fear and relief and . . . *pride.* The nest had never felt so joyful.

Several minutes passed.

Finally, Revver cleared his throat, and everyone quieted. "Mama," he said, "when I turn fifty days old, I'm going to live down there"—he pointed with his paw—"*at the speedway!*"

14

It was night forty-nine. Sprite was awake in the nest for a long time after everyone else had fallen asleep, looking up at the stars and listening to the sounds of Mama and her brothers breathing and snoring.

She sat up to look at Revver, cuddled between Farty's foot and Bounce's shoulder. There were tails here and there, but she could not tell whose was whose. They had all gotten so much bigger these past few weeks. It WAS getting crowded here. There was no doubt it was time for Sprite and her brothers to leave the nest. She knew that was true.

Sprite noticed that Revver still wore the chain

she had woven for him, tied around his furry ankle. For some reason, this made her want to smile and cry at the same time. Her chest felt tight.

"Revver," she whispered into his ear. But Revver was sound asleep. It didn't matter. She kept talking to him. "Revver, please stay safe. Try to slow down and think things through. Most importantly, just be safe. And be happy, too, Revver. I want you to be happy."

Sprite cuddled down into the nest next to Revver. This would be the last time they were all together like this. She tried to notice everything she could. She didn't want to forget: the sound of the leaves, her brothers breathing, the crickets chirping. She studied the stars and the moonlight through the branches above her. This was home, but only for one last night.

She took a deep breath of the night air and, of course, Farty let out a *pfooooof!* at that very moment. She held her nose. Tonight, that made her laugh. She giggled quietly and felt less sad and a little less worried.

Finally, she started to feel sleepy. She whispered one more time, "I won't be around to save you, Revver. So please, *please* be safe."

Sprite had no way of knowing that SHE might be the one who would need saving.

15

The sun had not even started to peek up.

"Hey," Bounce said, bolting up.

Silence.

"HEY!" he said louder, and he started jumping.

Still no answer.

"HEEEYYY!" This time he screamed and pounced, making the nest shake like a trampoline.

"Oh, *brother!* Hey, *what?*" answered a sleepy voice from deep down in the nest.

"IT'S TODAY!" yelled Bounce again.

"What's today?" said another sleepy voice, along with a little squeak of air.

"What's today?! WHAT'S TODAY?!" Bounce

huffed. "SERIOUSLY?! How could you forget?! We're fifty days! Today is SCURRY-AWAY DAY!"

"He's right! It's morning! It's TODAY!"

The children untangled themselves from under one another.

Mama had been out gathering berries. "Breakfast, dears! And happy birthday! Fifty days already! My oh my, time does fly!" she said.

Everyone was excited and chattered about their plans. After breakfast, it was time for the long-goodbye group huddle. Mama and her children sat in a circle in the nest. Five sets of paws stacked one on top of another, with one of Mama's paws on the bottom of the stack and her other paw on the top.

"Now, remember to stay safe. And report back to me often, and remember that we always keep an eye on one another . . ."

"We know! We know!"

"And don't forget your Essential Skills . . ."

"We know!"

A stink of air rose through the nest. "And, Farty, dear, do try to eat more slowly."

"Yes, Mama. So I can *request*!"

"It's *digest*, dear," Mama corrected. "And, Sprite, be careful and please try to keep an eye on the boys when you can."

Oh, brothers, thought Sprite, eager to be brother-free for a while.

"And, Revver, dear, for the life of me, I just cannot unders—"

"I know, Mama. No one understands. But it's okay! I'll be fine."

"Well, dear, do at least *try* to be careful around all those dangerous—"

"Mama, I know, I know!"

"Yes, well, okay, then. Good luck, my dears. Go ahead."

All together, four voices chanted, "*Aaaand* we're OFF!" as they raised their paws in the air in victory, cheering.

"*Vr-vr-vr-VRRROOOOM!*" went Revver, startling everyone.

"PLEASE. STOP . . . Oh wait. Never mind!" said Bounce. Everyone laughed as the four of them jumped out of the nest for the last time and ran their separate ways.

For just a moment, Sprite turned back to look at the other three, heading off in different directions.

"*Oh, brothers,*" she said. She smiled at them. This time, she was not one bit annoyed.

16

Revver sped off as fast as he could run. *Front paws, back paws, front paws, back paws.* He practically flew!

He was so deep in thought about his exciting, *fast* life ahead at the track that he ran right into it at full speed, and he was almost knocked out. When he shook himself off and slowly looked up, his mouth hung open with shock. There, like a huge beast, just waiting to end all his hopes and dreams, stood the WALL.

From their nest high in the tree, the wall that surrounded the track was barely noticeable. But once Revver faced it at ground level, he realized: IT WAS HUGE. Bigger than he'd ever imagined,

SO MUCH bigger than it looked from their old nest so far away. This would be a challenge.

Rising up, up, up from the ground was a tall mass of smooth, thick concrete. On top of the concrete stood metal fencing, a mesh of tight steel cables. On top of that was even MORE woven cable, bending inward toward the track at a dangerously sharp angle—ensuring that anything that flew around during a race would stay *in*. Or, in this case, making good and sure that a squirrel would stay *out*.

Revver ran long lengths of the wall, hoping for a just-right squirrel-size hole that he could squeeze through. He could not BELIEVE how big the track was! When he looked at it from the nest, he could cover each turn with his paw. But, up close, it was SO ENORMOUS!

He had no luck finding a way in. He ran the entire route a second time, just to be sure he didn't miss anything. Again, nothing. Sprite was probably small enough to fit between the links and, for a second, Revver thought about getting her to help. But what good would it be to get HER in if HE couldn't get in? Plus, he HAD to figure this out himself. He had something to prove.

He covered the same route again, but this time he crawled low along the ground. Maybe there was a hole at the bottom . . . or some way he could dig under? Nope.

By now, he had run MOST of the track several times. He was getting really, really tired.

Revver sat with his back against the wall and looked toward his old nest and tree. He felt homesick, which surprised him. The day had started out with such promise . . . He had expected that he'd already be living a life of speed and excitement at the track by now, and he had not even made it inside. He felt heavy with disappointment.

"*Vr-vr-vr-VROOM!*" he said to try to motivate himself. But it was a half-hearted effort.

Finally, he decided that the only way through this was OVER the wall.

He tried a fast running start and a big jump. His claws *almost* got a grip into the concrete, but he slid back down to the ground like slow-melting ice. He tried again. And again. He tried until he was panting and bruised from bashing his face into the wall on tries twelve and twenty-two.

This wasn't working. Trees were perfectly designed for squirrels. Or maybe squirrels were perfectly designed for trees. Either way, bark was rough, with lots of places for squirrel paws and claws to grab. And branches always seemed to come along at just the right place to help the climb. This wall was exactly UNLIKE a tree in every way. The concrete was too smooth. The steel cable was sharp, and the spaces between the metal links were awkward—a paw would easily slip right through.

He studied the wall more closely. Hmm, there were some tiny cracks and dents where he *might* be able to grab. He started up, carefully looking and deciding where to place the next paw. He had made it about halfway up when he missed and fell back to the ground, right onto his furry butt.

But Revver was determined. He tried again. He was almost to the top when he fell again.

On the sixth try, he finally made it to the catch fence. He began climbing up the links, slowly and carefully. At about halfway, he slipped and fell all the way back to the ground. It suddenly occurred to Revver that he might be much better at this if he had spent more time doing "squirrelly" things. He took a deep breath and started again from the beginning.

By evening, Revver had no more tries in him. He was more tired than he'd ever felt, and every muscle ached. Even his tail hurt from getting caught in the links during one of the falls.

He slumped against Turn One, picking up a few old nuts that had fallen there, and nibbled sadly. Then Revver buried his face in his paws. After a long time, he fell asleep.

17

Morning came, warm and sunny. Revver was still tired and sad. *Watching the cars might make me feel better*, he thought. Speed and power always brought him joy. He found a small crack between the concrete slabs, pressed one eye up against the wall, and settled in to watch.

There, something giant and black stared back at Revver, and it was coming right toward him, FAST! Then it blurred past him, growling a LOUD warning: *"Vruuuu-uuum!"* which he knew for sure meant, "STAY OUT!"

"Aaaaaaaaahhh!" Revver screamed. He jumped back from the wall and started running away, shaking with fear.

He ran and ran, and he didn't dare look back. A MONSTER AT THE TRACK! The monster KNEW that Revver was trying to get in! A squirrel-eating, track-guarding monster! *Why does it seem like EVERYTHING wants to eat squirrels?!*

Without thinking or even knowing why, Revver started sprinting toward the walnut tree, screaming, "Sprite!" as he ran. "Sprite! Sprite! Help me!"

He ran as fast as he could, checking back over his shoulder to make sure the monster wasn't following him. Then **SMACK!** he was on his side, curled up into a ball in pain.

Ughhhh!

He had crashed into the walnut tree trunk.

When he looked up, he saw Sprite sitting peacefully at the base of the tree, weaving something out of some long yellow stems. Revver was out of breath. "Mon-mon-mon-monster!" was all he could pant out.

"*Oh, brother, you're back already?*" said Sprite as she looked up. "*What now?*" She sighed, set down her weaving, and sat next to him to listen.

"At the t-t-t-track," Revver stammered. "M-monster! B-b-b-**BIG**!"

Revver finally calmed down enough to tell her everything—about the wall and the sad night he'd had. He told her about his morning, about seeing the monster staring him down and chasing him away. Sprite stood up.

"Okay, come on," she said, and she started tugging him by the wrist.

"Where?" he asked.

"Where do you think? The track!"

"No! I told you!"

"So what, then?"

"I guess I'll just stay here with you."

"No WAY, little brother. You HAVE to go back. You can't give up your dream."

He really hated when she called him that. She

could be such a know-it-all. He hated that, too. "I'm not going back."

"RIGHT NOW!" she yelled. He knew better than to question her when she used that voice with him. But she still had to practically drag him, using all her strength. "Come ON!" she scolded every once in a while as she pulled harder. Revver realized again, she was stronger than she looked.

Finally, they were back at the track, staring up at the wall.

"Now, think, Revver! **Stop and THINK!** Remember when you were going to jump into the nest from the top of our tree? How did the nest look to you from up there?"

Revver thought back to that day. He had to think for a long time, because it was hard to remember anything besides Sprite ruining his fun that day. He finally said, "It looked really small?"

"Right! YES! That's right! And what did you notice about this wall when you got to it yesterday?"

Revver thought hard again. "It was HUGE! SO MUCH bigger than I thought."

"Yes! Yes, that's right! Now, come here . . . Show me where you saw the monster."

"No." Revver took a seat and crossed his arms. He was NOT moving any closer.

"Revver, just point. I'll go look."

"Over there." He pointed.

Sprite went and pressed one eye to the crack between the concrete slabs at the corner. Revver heard the monster coming again! "Sprite!" he screamed. "Watch out!" But Sprite stood, calm. Revver was curled up, hiding his eyes. Sprite walked back over to her brother.

"Did you see it?! D-d-did you?! Did you see the monster?!"

"Revver! No! No, OF COURSE I didn't see it! Just stop! Just STOP AND THINK! You've NEVER seen a monster at the track before, have you? It's not a MONSTER, Revver." She put her hands on his shoulders and looked into his eyes. She spoke more softly. "Listen to me, Revver: It's. A. CAR!"

Revver's mouth hung open. He shook his head. He was very confused.

S-l-o-w-l-y, his confusion went away. Just like the wall, a car would look A LOT bigger to him from down here. And it would probably *sound* a lot different, too—a lot louder—when he was so much closer . . .

He stood up and slowly decided to look for himself. He pressed one eye against the crack of the wall. Sprite squeezed in under him. He heard the growling again. He reached out and grabbed Sprite's paw for safety. He forced himself to be brave and to keep his eyes open. Soon, he saw it, coming closer: the scary eyes and mouth—or maybe, on second look, it was just the front grill—coming closer and closer. It WAS, in fact, a car. But it *was* MONSTROUSLY HUGE.

He jumped back. He let out a little chuckle. "You know what, Sprite? I've changed my mind about this. I don't think the track is the place for me after all. Let's go."

Sprite gently turned him back. "Revver, you LOVE cars, remember?"

"I think . . . I might only love them from far away."

"Little brother, I've been hearing about the track since we were three days old! I'm not letting you back out now. IT'S YOUR DREAM."

"But, but—"

"Nuh-uh. Nope. Never. No WAY. Now, get in THERE."

"Okay, well, even if I COULD get in there . . ."

"Of COURSE you can get in there!"

"Sprite! I already told you . . ."

"About?"

"The WALL!"

"Revver: STOP and THINK. How big are you?"

Revver rubbed himself from his head to his feet. "THIS big," he said.

"And how big was that car you just saw?"

"HUGE! GIANT! GINORMOUS!"

She held each of his wrists and shook him. "Now, again: STOP and THINK. If that GIANT car could get into the track . . ."

Revver felt like he'd been *zapped*! "The CARS!" He jumped and screamed. "Of *course*!"

He felt so stupid! It was so obvious! If there was

a way for all those BIG CARS to get in, there was DEFINITELY a way in for someone his size! He hadn't looked far enough! He hadn't thought hard enough! He hadn't gone completely around the ENTIRE track!

"Okay?"

"Okay!"

"All good?"

"All good!"

"Okay, Revver. I think you can take it from here. I'm going home." Sprite started back toward the walnut tree.

"Sprite! Wait!"

"Revver, you'll be fine. It's okay."

"No, that's not it."

"What *now*, then?"

"It's just that . . ." Revver ran toward Sprite, picked her up, and hugged her tightly. "Thank you, Sprite," he whispered. "Thank you."

Even Revver had to admit that being Sprite's "little brother" was a good thing sometimes.

18

He felt light as air as he started the trek around the outside of the fence—around Turn One and toward Turn Two, where he had turned around yesterday. But he kept going, scurrying to get there as fast as he could.

And there, beneath Turn Two, he saw THE TUNNEL! The tunnel led under the track and right into the infield. *Of course!* From the nest, he'd seen long lines of trucks and trailers coming into the track from here, almost as if they'd magically appeared from underground.

He thought of yesterday, and he was so angry at himself for not taking the time to stop and think! Right then and there, Revver knew he needed to start keeping important ideas that might help him out later. He thought awhile. *Near the nest, Mama had scratched out a hole in the tree trunk—a "burrow"—to hold food for safekeeping. That's exactly what I need!* Revver decided. He closed his eyes and cleared out a little hollow in his brain.

Then he put his first important idea, **Stop and think**, right into his brain burrow. He thought over the last few days, and he remembered the scene with the hawk. He thought of another idea, **Revving is good!** and he safely tucked that idea away, too.

Now he sat near the base of the tunnel, waiting and watching. A truck drove up to the gate. The truck was REALLY ENORMOUS! Just like Sprite said, *things looked a lot bigger once you got close to them.* Revver had to force himself to watch and to be brave, because the size and sound of the truck REALLY made him want to run and hide. Revver held steady.

The driver stopped, opened his window, and waited. A human was standing at the gate, and he went over to talk to the driver. The driver showed him something, and the guard went back to his station and opened the gate. Revver watched carefully as two more trucks did the same thing.

Revver took a deep breath for courage. When the next truck got to the gate, Revver waited until the guard was busy talking to that driver; then he ran to the opposite side of the guard stand. When the guard opened the gate, Revver took another deep breath and ran through, unnoticed.

At last, Revver was in.

19

He found his way through the infield and toward the track. From a safe spot behind the inside wall, Revver peeked over and watched the car. He felt the familiar tingle in his insides when he saw it! It WAS so much bigger than he'd expected! But being this close to it was so much BETTER than he had expected, too. He could feel the vibrations of the engine through his whole small self.

The car squealed off and zipped around the track for some practice laps. When it came in, the crew jumped into action with some quick adjustments and then sent the car back out for more testing.

Revver watched everything. Every. Single. Thing. He stopped feeling afraid and started feeling really, REALLY excited.

After a few more laps, the driver slowed and headed to the nearby garage and shut off the engine.

Revver ran to follow, being sure to stay hidden. The driver lowered the net, slipped out of the window, and removed his helmet. He stood around the car with the crew chief and the rest of the team. So many humans all gathered around the car, all talking about the car, all caring about the car . . . Revver suddenly had a terrible longing to be a part of that group.

The humans moved away from the car and huddled together, still talking. Some motioned with their hands. Some talked. Some nodded. Every once in a while, Revver could make out a word, like "loose" or "vibration."

None of the crew members were looking at the car. Without even thinking, Revver jumped closer.

He was right next to it now!

It was BIG.

It was BEAUTIFUL!

Now that he was so close, he could almost reach out and touch it. He had never touched a car before! It was so colorful and shiny, so wonderful . . .

He felt very brave. He did NOT "stop and think." His thoughts were speeding too quickly around his brain. The car was not moving, so it certainly could not flatten him! It seemed very safe. He just wanted to touch it. Just. One. Little. Touch.

He scurried toward the side of the car and took a moment to take in the full view. His mouth hung open as his eyes looked up at the glorious machine.

He rubbed his paws gently over the colorful decals. He got braver. He pressed himself up against the side of the car with his arms out wide, giving the car a big, long hug, so he could feel as much as he could, all at once.

"Wooow," he whispered in awe.

He jumped over toward the driver's side window opening, running his paws along the car the entire way. He tried to look inside, but it was too high. He tried jumping up and down to get a better view, but he could not see much.

*I **need** to see inside!*

Revver hurried back to the front of the car. He jumped on the bumper and then onto the lid. ***Ouch-ouch-ouch-ouch!*** The lid was fiery hot! Revver nearly burned his paws! *The rumbly-ma-jingy thingy gets HOT!* This was new news. Trying not to yelp, he jumped onto the roof and quickly flattened himself to avoid being seen. Then he inched back over toward the driver's side and looked inside, hanging upside down from the roof.

The steering wheel, the controls, the shifter—they were all unfamiliar to him. "So THIS is how they make it work! *Awesome!*" he whispered again. He quickly thought about the car he had tried to make. *I didn't have a circle-stick in my car! I have a lot to learn . . .*

He leaned over to see more . . . leaning, leaning, leaning . . . until he started to slip off the smooth roof. His head dangled above the driver's seat now, but his rear paw was tangled in the window net.

"*Errrrrrr-err!*" With some grunting and twisting, Revver quickly untangled himself and fell onto the seat, head and front paws first. He righted himself onto his back paws. It took him a few moments to really realize where he was.

I'm INSIDE a real race car! I'm here! I'm really here! He could feel his heart pounding right up through his ears. His insides felt electric and excited.

With his back paws on the seat, he was able to place the very tips of his front paws onto the lowest part of the steering wheel. *"Vroooom-vroom!"* he said quietly, pretending to drive.

He jumped onto the floor to admire the pedals, and touched them gently, with great respect. *These must be important, too!* he thought. He was just starting to put the pieces together. Then he jumped back onto the seat to feel the shifter with his paws.

He was so excited that he did not notice the crew coming back toward the car.

20

Someone opened the lid to inspect inside. Just in time, Revver jumped out of sight behind the driver's seat and tucked into a tiny, tight space between the roll cage bars and seat.

In a blink, the driver was harnessed back in the seat, the net was back up, and one of the crew members slammed the lid shut. The driver started the engine—and it roared like thunder.

Revver had no time to think! He pressed his back against the metal behind him and braced himself with his paws. He was headed out of the garage and back onto the track.

The driver pulled onto the track and picked up speed, faster, faster, and faster. The turn pushed

Revver into the corner of the car, and the force held him there tightly. When the car straightened, the intense speed pressed so hard on the little squirrel that he was sure he would fly right through the back of the car.

The sound! The shaking! The speed! His ears, his whiskers, every strand of his fur, and even his paws were all plastered back. His mouth was in the shape of a huge O. His eyes were opened wide in fear. His memories flashed: He remembered falling out of the nest. He remembered the hawk. He remembered seeing the giant, angry monst— Well, he remembered seeing the car through the wall for the first time. Those times, he had been SCARED. Now, he was TERRIFIED.

But something began to happen after the first, frightening lap. Revver began to relax. He started to focus on what was happening. The more he paid attention, the more excited he became. His insides quivered! By the third lap, his excitement had turned into pure *joy*. "I can't believe it! I'm here! I'm really here! I'm racing! I'm *fast*!" He was screaming! He wanted to jump for joy, but the force of the speed had him pressed hard against the back of the car.

His excitement had been welling up since the moment he first touched the car, and by the start of lap five, he could not hold it in a second more: **"Vr-vr-vr-VRRROOOOM!"**

The driver quickly downshifted and slowed. Revver fell forward, right onto his nose, and scurried to hide himself again. The driver said into his headset, "It was running great, but now it's making a really weird sound, and I just heard a little thump. I'm gonna bring 'er in so you can take a quick look."

"Uh-oh," Revver whispered under the engine noise.

The driver brought the car back into the garage. The crew chief spoke to the driver through the window opening. Revver tried to make himself as small as possible behind the seat, with a metal can helping to hide him.

Finally, the driver turned off the engine, pulled

off the steering wheel, lowered the window net, and slipped out of the window opening. Revver could hear him talking to the crew chief. "Maybe it was just some feedback on the radio," he heard. "It was lookin' awfully good out there." Revver, despite himself, nodded with excitement, as best as a squirrel can nod.

Revver jumped onto the driver's seat and slowly peeked up for a look. Everyone seemed to have their backs to the car. *Here's my chance!* He leapt out the window and ran under the car for another peek. "Clear!" he whispered again as he ran, full speed, out of the garage, to a hiding spot behind the garage wall.

Once he was under cover, Revver patted himself from the top of his head to the tips of his toes to the end of his furry tail. "Not even a tiny bit flat!" he pronounced.

He was safe. For now.

21

Revver sat outside, against the garage wall. He replayed the last few exciting moments in his mind, again and again. He could hardly believe they had really happened!

The growling of his stomach broke his concentration. "I guess I've missed breakfast! *And lunch!*" He was about to head toward some trees in the infield garage area to find something to eat, but a sound interrupted his thoughts and made him curious.

He peeked through the door opening to see. In another part of the garage, a young man was doing something very interesting. A wheel was mounted to a panel, and the man held a special tool against five bright-yellow pieces inside, turning them magically: *zhhht-zhhht-zhhht-zhhht-zhhht!*

"*Ooooh!*" He sat and stared, mesmerized. *He's working on the go-a-rounds!* Revver forgot all about being hungry as he watched the man working.

Zhhht-zhhht-zhhht-zhhht-zhhht!—five times fast. Then a break. Then again. *Zhhht-zhhht-zhhht-zhhht-zhhht!* And again.

The human stood tall to stretch. Out of the corner of his eye, he caught a glimpse of Revver standing in the doorway. They stared at each other, but neither of them moved.

"Hey, fella," the man finally said in a soft, slow voice, "whatcha doin' in here?"

Revver watched the man carefully. The man looked at Revver. Then the man let out a little laugh. "You're awfully cute, aren't ya?" Revver kept watching. He was ready to run away if things turned scary.

"*Hmm,*" the man said, still looking at Revver, "lemme see what I've got here . . ." The man dug into the pocket of his coveralls. "Do ya like peanuts? I've got some here." The man moved very slowly and very carefully toward Revver. He placed something on the shiny white floor of the garage entrance and slowly backed away.

Revver did not move. He kept his eyes on the human. Finally, Revver took a few steps closer and sniffed the object. It smelled *delicious*. His stomach growled again. Carefully, Revver nibbled. It *tasted* delicious! Now he felt braver. With caution, he moved closer to the man.

The man laughed again. "Ya like those, huh? Have ya had peanuts before? Okay, fella, here's a couple more." The man set two more little objects in front of Revver and, this time, Revver ate them without hesitating.

The human carefully came closer to Revver and kneeled in front of him. Revver stayed on guard, watching to see what would happen, still ready to run. The man s-l-o-w-l-y moved his hand toward Revver and gently rubbed the top of Revver's head and behind his ears. It felt so good— like when Mama or Sprite rubbed his ears. Revver felt safe. He leaned in for more petting. "Well, I'll be darned," the man whispered, laughing a little again. "Aren't you *somethin'*?"

After a while, the man slowly stood up. "Well, buddy, I gotta get back to work. You better scat out now, 'fore someone sees ya." The man gently nudged Revver toward the door. Revver went outside but did not go far. He peeked in through the door crack again, watching while the man went back to working. The noise started up again: *zhhht-zhhht-zhhht-zhhht-zhhht!* Revver could not stop watching the man work.

Suddenly Revver heard a loud *CLUNK!* as something sparked against the floor and bounced high, nearly hitting the man in the face before bouncing away.

"Nuts," the man grumbled.

The squirrel awoke from his trance and gulped. **"NUTS?!"** Revver suddenly realized that he was still VERY hungry. Without stopping to think, he quickly chased after what had fallen.

With a jolt, he caught it and popped it right

into his mouth. It sat on his tongue for a moment. No nutty sweetness. Cold . . . and way too hard. *Hmm . . .* , he thought. **Not** acorn. **Not** walnut. **Not** peanut . . .

Immediately, Revver knew he'd made a big mistake. He had not remembered to smell it first! He started to choke! He was panicking. Finally, he coughed and spit it out onto the floor. *Clank!*

The man, whose concentration had been broken by the ruckus, started laughing. He walked over to Revver, who continued to stare at the object on the floor. The man knelt down and picked up the runaway object in his gloved hand.

"Not the kind of nut you expected, eh? This is a LUG nut, friend," the man said, chuckling. He had such a kind voice.

LUG. NUT. Revver paid attention to the words.

"Ya don't wanna eat THOSE, that's for sure! Made of metal and all. But *whew*! That was a mighty fine bit of fetching! What brings you here to the track, little guy? Are you a racin' fan?"

Revver nodded, as best as a squirrel can nod.

The man had never seen a squirrel—or any animal—nod. It was, as best as he could tell, a very HUMAN kind of nod.

The man jumped back in surprise. "Whoa!" The man stood and thought quietly for a very long time. Finally, he asked softly, a little afraid, "Can you understand me, little dude?"

Revver nodded again.

"WHOA!" the man shouted again, but this time VERY LOUDLY.

The shout brought several other crew members rushing over. "What's goin' on, Bill? You okay?!" one of them asked.

"U-um," Bill stuttered, "I'm, I'm, I'm not sure y'all will believe this!"

The crew looked at Bill and followed Bill's eyes down to the floor to look at Revver. Revver looked up at everyone.

22

"We'll never believe that a squirrel got into the garage?" one of the crew asked, chuckling as he chewed something.

"Yeah, that's UNBELIEVABLE, Bill. Call the reporters, quick!" Now everyone was chuckling.

"No, no, no, not that. Now, listen, this is gonna sound strange, but just listen. I SWEAR that this critter can understand what I'm saying to him," said Bill.

Everyone laughed again.

"Hilarious, Bill! What's the joke?"

"No, no joke—I'm not kidding. I'm serious. I mean, I think I am. I mean, *maybe . . .*"

"Bill, *maybe* the fumes are gettin' to ya," one man said, and everyone laughed again.

"Wait," Bill said. "Y'all just watch this." Then Bill knelt down again, facing Revver. "Okay, buddy, tell the crew here: Are you a racing fan?"

Revver nodded again, a very HUMAN kind of nod.

A wave of surprise went through the crew.

"NO way!"

"Holy smokes!"

"That did NOT just happen!"

"Well, I'll BE!"

"Wait a minute, Bill. This is some kind of *trick*, right? How'd you do it?"

"Dude, I promise you, I just met this critter when he came in a few minutes ago. I haven't had time to teach him any tricks."

Someone said, "All right, well, maybe it's just a coincidence. Ask him somethin' else."

"Okay," Bill said, still kneeling in front of Revver. "Little fella, do you like nuts?"

Revver nodded again.

"Well, I'll be DARNED." A woman's voice spoke up this time. "I'll admit, that's a little weird!"

"Wait. Maybe he nods to everything you ask 'im. Ask 'im a 'no' question."

"Oh, good idea. Okay. Hmm." Bill thought a moment. Then he looked back down to Revver and said, "Well, okay, do you like, uhh . . ." Bill kept thinking. "Bears?" he said finally.

Revver shook his head quickly. That was a definite *no*—a very HUMAN *no*!

"If we weren't all seeing this together, I'd think the fumes *might* be gettin' to ME!"

"I see it, but I'm not sure I even believe it!"

"Maybe we're ALL goin' a little nutty?" said one of the men.

"Well, YOU are, but that's nothin' new." Everyone laughed again.

Revver did not understand the joke, so he just looked around at all the faces.

"Maybe he's hungry," someone suggested.

Bill reached into his pocket, pulled out another peanut, and handed it to the little squirrel, who sat on his hind legs. Revver eagerly took it and crunched away. Others handed him other things to try, but this time Revver remembered to sniff each new thing. He took a potato chip, a baby carrot, and a small piece of a candy bar. Someone gave him the crust off a peanut butter sandwich, which Revver found DELIGHTFUL, but it made his mouth awfully dry and sticky. He tried to clear the peanut butter from the top of his mouth, making loud clicking noises.

"Give the poor guy somethin' to drink," another voice spoke out.

Bill had a green bottle with a colorful label sitting nearby. He took a small cap and filled it with the liquid.

Revver approached the cap cautiously. He tried hard to remember: How DID a squirrel know if water was safe to drink? He thought and thought, trying hard to remember. Then, deep down in his memory, he heard his mother's voice from Squirrel School: *The rules are* look *and* smell. *You should be able to see through it. It should look fresh and smell tasty.* He remembered!

He looked. The liquid had a slight color, but he

could see through it. He smelled it, and it smelled sweet and good, but it made a strange fizzy sound. Hmm . . . He wasn't sure, but his mouth felt miserably sticky. He was getting desperate.

Bill's voice said, "Go ahead, fella. It's okay." For some reason, Revver just *knew* he could trust this man they called "Bill."

Revver took a teeny, tiny taste. It was sweet. It was DELICIOUS! Immediately, Revver gulped down the rest, and Bill quickly refilled the cap four more times. Revver quickly finished each serving, bubbles and all.

"There you go, buddy. Feel better?" asked Bill.

Revver started to nod, but, instead, a long, loud, satisfied **BURP!** came out of him.

The crew broke out laughing.

"Well, he certainly fits in with this group!"

Revver, not too sure of what had just happened, looked around at the laughing group and smiled, as best as a squirrel can smile.

"I think we'll just stick to water from now on, bud," Bill said to Revver.

There were some scattered giggles, and then Bill asked, almost afraid of the answer, "Okay, little guy, um, you can't *talk* or anything, can you?"

Revver spoke up immediately. "Of course I can talk! I'm a SQUIRREL! Can we talk about RACING?! I just LOVE racing! My mother and my sister and brothers think cars are DANGEROUS, but I think they are AMAZING and EXCITING and just, so, so **FAST**! I love everything fast! The size of them took some getting used to! Well, you understand, right? No one ever understands, but I think YOU just might because, well, you know . . ." Revver inhaled and continued. "So please tell me all about cars! I have so much to learn. They seem so amaz . . ."

Revver stopped to look at the man's face, and then he looked around at all the others and saw only confused looks. He realized that, although he could clearly understand Human, humans were hopeless at understanding Squirrel.

Bill started to chuckle and ran his hand through his hair. He said to the crew, "Well, that's a relief, right, y'all? They'd have had us to the medic in about two seconds flat if we said we had a talking squirrel in the garage!"

Everyone laughed.

"Okay," said Bill, "how about this: Do you have a name—you know, somethin' we could call you?"

Revver nodded again enthusiastically, as best as a squirrel can nod.

"Okay," the man said, "well, I'm Bill, and that there is Jeff, and that's Susan, and that's Ashley, and that big dude there is Trevor, and that goofball there is Brandon, and that guy over there is Doug . . ." One by one, Bill introduced the entire crew.

Revver looked around at each person as Bill introduced them, trying to memorize their names and faces. He wasn't sure what any of the names meant, but he was very relieved that no one was named Farty.

"So help us out: How 'bout your name . . . ? What should we call you?"

Revver steadied himself, planted his feet firmly on the floor, took in a deep breath, and from deep within the little squirrel came the GIGANTIC, BOOMING, **"Vr-vr-vr-VRRROOOOM!"**

Everyone jumped back in surprise.

"Holy tailpipes!" someone yelled.

The whole group stared at the little creature standing on the shiny floor of the garage.

Bill asked gently, "Little fella, can you do that again?"

Revver nodded and once again ROARED—loud enough to vibrate the garage floor.

"Is that your name?" Bill asked.

Revver nodded, as best as a squirrel can nod.

"Well, now, I have no idea how to say that, buddy. That's more like a sound effect than a name. Sounds like you're revving a car. You're a little revver!"

Revver nodded wildly, better than any squirrel had ever nodded.

"What? Revver? Does that name sound about right for ya, little guy?"

Revver bounded over to Bill's feet and nodded again.

"Okay, little guy, um, Revver— it's nice to know you." Bill moved closer to the squirrel and whispered, "Hey, can we show 'em what else you can do?" as he held up a lug nut.

Revver nodded again as Bill tossed a lug nut high, toward the ceiling. Revver immediately leapt, caught the nut in midair, and dropped it down gently at Bill's feet.

Amid the oohs and aahs, the squirrel stood on his hind legs and looked around at the crew in amazement. There Revver stood, the center of attention, right in the middle of a real race team.

The crew was awestruck. And so was Revver.

23

"All right, folks," Bill said. "Race day's comin' quick. We gotta get back to work."

"So what are we gonna do with him?" Trevor asked Bill, pointing down at Revver. "You want me to grab a broom and shoo him out?"

"Can't we keep him round? He's awfully sweet," someone answered.

"Oh, right! Big Jack would just love that!" said someone else. "He'd welcome a rodent hanging around his team, messin' things up."

Revver was not sure what a *rodent* was, but it did not sound like something good. Revver, eyes filled with hope, looked up at Bill.

Someone else spoke up. "Bill, how many times

have we heard Jack say, 'No fur or filth allowed. This is a spotless operation!' He won't even let his own family dog in here!"

Bill ran his hand through his hair as he looked down at Revver. "Well, he might not mess things up too badly . . ."

Laughing, Susan pointed at the floor behind Revver. "I suppose ole Jack would be thrilled with squirrel turds all over his shiny floor, then."

Sure enough, Revver had dropped a few in all the excitement.

Bill bent over toward Revver and pointed at the poop. "Any chance you might be able to try to keep this OUTside?" Revver looked and sniffed. He studied the issue carefully. Surely he could remember not to poop in the garage! Revver nodded quickly as he thought hard . . . He added another note to his brain burrow: No pooping in the garage.

Bill continued. "Tell ya what, then. I'll make you a deal, Revver. How 'bout if I put you to work for a while? If you pick up the lugs I drop and bring 'em back to me, I'll trade ya for these." He dug into his pocket and pulled out a peanut. "That'll save me from having to sweep *these* up later," he said, holding up the lug nut with his other hand. Bill gently set down the big, salty, delicious peanut. Revver did not hesitate to take the peanut and nibble.

"Does that sound like a job for you?" Bill asked.

Revver could not believe his pointy little ears! He had a job! With a race team! He did, in fact, have a VALUABLE SKILL! It was more than he had ever imagined! *Who'd have thought it? I am perfectly suited for an actual JOB at the track! Fetching NUTS! Well, maybe not the kind of nuts I usually fetch, but a nut is a nut is a nut, right?!*

Revver nodded, as best as a squirrel can nod, to make sure that Bill understood that this sounded like a fine arrangement.

"And no more poopin' in here, right?"

Revver looked very serious. He shook his head to say no.

"Wow, that is SOME special squirrel," someone said.

Then everyone started talking at once.

"If Jack finds out about this, he'll have a fit."

"Well," said Bill, "I'm not sure how the team owner could be upset with a helper who works *for peanuts!*"

Everyone laughed.

"Seriously, though, Bill, if that squirrel gets into any trouble, Jack will have our heads. Remember his rule: NO ANIMALS, and NO PETS around the cars. You're flirting with danger here."

"But he's so smart! And he can help."

"I vote we let him stay around."

"And just look at him! He's such a cute little fella! He doesn't look like he could ever cause any trouble, does he?"

24

Revver and Bill got right to work.

Revver sat, concentrating hard. Whenever a lug nut dropped, Revver pounced and caught it. He gathered them up into a pile, and, every once in a while, Bill would pick them off the floor and reward his furry helper with a big handful of peanuts.

Revver learned to slide on the shiny white floor. With a running start from several feet away, he could catch the nut in the air as he slid to a stop. He loved that fast, breezy feeling!

Before long, Revver was an expert at fast slides and high jumps in pursuit of each precious lug

nut. *Bounce and Sprite would be so proud!* Revver thought. Bill was definitely impressed. He would catch a glimpse and say "Wow" or "Nice move" or "You got some real speed that time, fella!" Revver smiled to himself.

Revver wanted to go *faster*. This time, he backed WAY up for a long running start. When he saw the lug nut pop into the air, he began running toward it at full speed. Then he planted his two back feet flat on the floor and began to slide. He raised his paws high into the air, preparing to catch the nut.

But somewhere along the way, one back paw found the tiniest drop of motor oil on the smooth floor—and before he realized what was happening, Revver was facing the wrong way, flipping and flailing. He tried to keep his eyes on the nut so he could still make the catch, but there was no hope.

He barrel-rolled before finally coming to a stop, headfirst and facedown, at Bill's feet, with all four paws and his tail spread out wide.

Bill picked Revver up from the floor by the scruff and looked him in the eyes to see if the squirrel was okay—and a lug nut flew out of Revver's mouth and **SMACK!** hit Bill on the forehead, right between his eyes.

Bill rubbed the small bump the lug nut had made and said, "Again? Dude! I told you before: you don't want to be eatin' those!"

Revver saw the red mark on Bill's face. Bill sounded angry. Revver's heart sank and words began spilling out: "Oh no! I'm so sorry! I didn't mean to . . . I was going too fast . . ."

Revver shut his eyes and braced for the worst. Probably, Bill was going to eat him.

But nothing happened.

Revver opened his eyes and faced a puzzled-looking Bill.

"You remember I have no idea what you're saying, right? Hey, don't look so upset. Are you worried you're going to get fired?" Bill laughed.

Revver screamed, "**Set me on FIRE?!** Is that what you do?! Oh my word! That sounds worse than being eaten!"

Bill looked at Revver. "Hey, relax, dude; I was kidding! It's no big deal, bud. Accidents happen. Making mistakes . . . that's how we learn. Got it?"

Revver nodded, relieved. He made mistakes all

the time! Learning from them was SO much better than getting eaten for them! This felt like something that needed to be remembered. Inside his brain he thought, Learn from mistakes, and he tucked the idea away for safekeeping.

Bill put Revver back on the ground, and they both got back to work—Revver caught lug nut after lug nut and ate peanut after peanut. It was happy work.

After a while, Susan came over to Bill. "Hey, Bill, I have an idea. Can you bring that critter and take a look at someth—" Then she saw the big mark over Bill's eye. "Holy smokes, what *happened?*"

"Just a lug that got away." Bill rubbed the bump and winked at Revver. Revver was grateful that Bill, like Sprite, could keep a secret. "Whatcha need?"

"Just somethin' I thought Revver might be able to help us out with . . ."

Revver followed Susan and Bill around a partition to A CAR! It was RIGHT THERE, bright, shiny, and beautiful! Revver ran ahead of them and wrapped his arms around one of the front *go-a-rounds*, hugging it hard.

Bill and Susan watched him. Susan looked confused. Bill looked at Susan and shrugged. "I guess he likes tires."

Tires! Revver had another new word. *Go-a-rounds* were called *tires!*

Some crew members were standing around the car, talking to one another. Something BIG hung in the air above the front of the car.

"Where's your squirrel?" one of them asked when he saw Bill. Bill pulled Revver quickly off the tire he was still hugging, and lifted him up. They stood around the car with the others.

There, dangling in the air, was something BEAUTIFUL. It took Revver a few moments to realize what it was. In the strangest way, it looked a little like something Sprite might weave together out of all sorts of different things. Everything fit together perfectly. He noticed all the twisty parts and pieces, and finally he understood! His mouth hung open: it was the *rumbly-ma-jingy thingy*! He wanted to touch it but was afraid it would be hot.

Bill looked at him and somehow understood. "It's okay, Revver. You can touch the engine if you want."

Ohhh! The *rumbly-ma-jingy thingy* was *the* **ENGINE**! *A real, live* **drivers-start-your-engines** ENGINE! Revver thought he must be dreaming. He touched a small piece of the metal carefully, but it was not hot this time. In fact, it felt a little cold. There was so much to learn. Revver wanted so badly to understand it all.

He raised his paw and pointed to the thing holding the engine up in the air. He looked at Bill, hopeful for answers. "That's the *engine hoist*," Bill said, and Revver nodded to show Bill that he wanted to know all the words.

Then he watched closely as the engine hoist, *smoothly and carefully*, lowered the engine into the car, guided by some of the crew.

Revver peeked in. *The engine!* It took his breath away! He looked at all the strange, beautiful shapes; the shiny metal parts; the twisting tubes and colorful wires. Everything looked special and strong and important. Revver studied it all as hard as he could. He just knew: he was looking deep into the heart of the car. He thought back to the twigs and the angry bee he had used to make his own car engine. He first felt very foolish, but then he remembered his latest note, learn from mistakes. Revver was already learning SO MUCH.

"So, little guy . . ." Susan cleared her throat. "Um, you understand me, right?" she asked.

Revver nodded like crazy.

"Wow, this is weird. But okay, so we're wondering . . . Do you think you could help us with something? Since you've got those tiny paws and you can fit into tight spots and all, we were thinking that you might be able to help us with some *wiring*."

Revver had no idea what *wiring* was. He had no idea what he'd have to do, but he didn't care! All he KNEW was that he'd be learning and helping! He was here with a real race car with a real race team, and he might have ANOTHER skill to help.

A **"Vr-vr-vr-VRRROOOOM!"** roared out of Revver in excitement.

Suddenly a booming voice shouted, "What the Sam heck was *that*?!"

Bill quickly leaned over, grabbed Revver, and hid him behind his back. No one said anything.

The voice shouted again, "I *said*, WHAT WAS THAT?!"

"Oh, hey, Jack. We didn't hear you there."

Jack! Revver thought, *the team owner!* Revver felt nervous and stayed very still behind Bill's back.

Doug stuttered, "U-um, sorry, Jack. That was just, um, me. I was . . . just, uh . . . singing."

"Well, it's horrible! Don't give up your day job. Everything okay in here?"

"Oh sure, just working away."

"Yep."

"All good."

"Yes, sir."

"Good," said the team owner. "Keep at it." And he walked away.

Revver decided that he did NOT like Jack.

"Whoa, that was close. You gotta be careful, Revver; we don't want Jack to toss you outta here."

"Or worse."

Revver wasn't sure what *worse* was, but he was pretty sure it would have *something* to do with being eaten or set on fire. And just as scary: *I almost lost my chance to stay with the team!* Revver's heart was beating fast. He went into his brain burrow and took out one of the notes: Revving is good! Then he added the word SOMETIMES.

Then the team got back to work, so Revver did too. He listened to the instructions from Susan and the others and carefully fed wires through tubes and into places, just as he was instructed. Revver tucked himself deep into the engine, under pedals inside the car, and around the wheel wells just as he was asked. As he worked, he learned. The wires moved power to different places in the car. Everything in the car was connected to everything else in some way. It was a fascinating idea. Revver felt that the idea might be important enough to save, so he put the thought safely into his burrow: Everything is connected to everything else.

When he finished each task, someone handed him something delicious: he tasted apple, grapes, something called "cookie," and delightful little things called "M&M's." He also learned he was not a big fan of "jerky," which reminded him of tree bark.

Revver was surrounded by friends, friends who loved cars and racing as much as he did. Finally, he was with others who *understood*! They knew that racing and cars and being fast were IMPORTANT. This, THIS was why he wanted to leave the trees and live at the track! For the first time, Revver felt something different . . . He thought hard. He tried to put a name to this strange new feeling . . . At last, he decided it was *happy*. Revver was happy.

That night, Revver cuddled in a corner of the garage with a pile of clean shop towels that Bill had fluffed up to make Revver a nice, comfy little bed. Revver was thinking and smiling, not quite able to believe it all. In the quiet, Revver thought all about the adventures of the past day: getting into the track and riding in the race car and all the work he'd done. He could LEARN THINGS. He was HELPFUL. He was USEFUL. He had SKILLS, *important skills*. He was part of the team.

He thought a lot about the wiring. He thought about how things were all connected, and he wondered if that might be true for things besides cars.

He wished so badly that his brothers, and especially Sprite, were cuddled around him so he could tell them all about everything he'd done. And even Mama, who was always so frustrated by Revver in Squirrel School, would be so impressed by how much he could learn.

The longer Revver thought, the more he realized: even though he felt so happy, way deep down, there was the littlest feeling of sadness. Revver missed his family.

26

The team worked hard preparing for race day. Revver helped wherever he was needed. Along the way, he kept learning. He learned and learned.

There was so much more to cars and racing than what he had seen from the nest! He learned about the "chassis" and the "body." He learned that the lid that covered the engine was really called a "hood." And there was "fuel." Fuel was very important! He learned about "pit stops." He could see pit stops from the nest, but he could never understand what was happening. During a pit stop on race day, filling the car with fuel was one person's ONLY JOB! They called that person "fuel man," but they also called him Doug. Revver knew now that "Doug" and "fuel man" meant the same thing. Revver learned that "air" was as important for the car as fuel. But there was no "air man." Revver was still trying to understand that part.

Bill and the crew taught Revver everything they could while he watched them work. Each time they gave him a new word or explained something new to him, Revver would nod hard. He wanted to show them how much he liked to know new things.

The team chatted and whistled and laughed while they worked. Sometimes, while Revver watched them work, he would point to something with his paw. Then whoever was closest would say something like, "That's the 'crank shaft.' It turns the 'gears' and makes the car go." Revver would nod. Little by little, Revver started to understand.

Revver learned how the fuel and the air mixed together to create a little explosion inside the engine that made it move. He learned words like "fuel injector" and "cylinder." He learned about "rods" and "crankshafts" and "gears" and "transmission" and "exhaust" . . .

He learned that Bill was also called "tire changer" and that he was very strong and *very fast* at his job. Revver just loved that about Bill! He learned Bill's *zhhht-zhhht-zhhht-zhhht-zhhht* tool was called a "thunder gun." Or sometimes they called it an "impact wrench." Revver was not sure why some things—like Doug and Bill and Bill's tool—got two names. But he tried to remember all the words.

Humans sometimes had many words for the same thing. He learned the names of all the crew members, but he was sometimes confused when they were also called things like "Doofus" or "Wise Guy" or "Dork" . . . And sometimes "Doofus" or "Wise Guy" or "Dork" were DIFFERENT PEOPLE! This was confusing. Revver just kept paying attention, trying to figure it all out.

As race day got closer and closer, each new day felt busier. Once, Bill snuck Revver under his jacket and took him along to pit road, where Revver could watch the action on the track during qualifying.

Revver stayed low and out of sight so the team owner would not see him.

He could see and understand so much more than he could from the nest! Revver laughed when he remembered how scared he had been when he saw his first car. Now he could even laugh at himself when he thought about how he had tried to build his own car!

Watching the crew at work was amazing. When the car would pull into pit road, someone would quickly check over the tires while another someone would hand the driver a water bottle and someone else would wipe off the nose of the car and clean the windshield. It all happened at lightning speed!

Back in the garage, the crew practiced for race day. Revver watched jackman, tire changers, tire carriers, fuel guy—all jumping into action at just the right time, working together perfectly. Revver realized that each one played an important part in making the car go, everyone working together for a win. *Everything is connected to everything else,* he thought again.

Revver continued helping—picking up lug nuts for Bill or doing other little jobs just right for a little creature with little paws. *I'm part of the team.* It made Revver proud when he thought about that.

Now and again, someone would whistle or cough to let everyone know that the team owner was around and they needed to get Revver out of sight. Before lunch, Bill had to quickly toss Revver inside a stack of tires to hide him. Revver sat there for ten minutes (which felt like a very, VERY long time) while the team owner watched the crew, pointed his finger at things, and barked out instructions.

*How can anyone be so GRUMPY when they get to be around racing and **these fast cars** every single day?* It just made no sense to Revver. And he did not like the way Jack talked to his friends. It reminded him A LOT of how Sprite sounded when she scolded him.

Despite Grumpy Jack, Revver was happier than he ever remembered being—even watching racing from the old nest never made him feel this joyful. He was grateful for Bill and the crew. They were starting to feel more and more like a new family. Being around them and the cars was beginning to feel like home. Everyone worked hard, but they always had time to scratch Revver behind his ears, show him something new, let him help with the work, or give him a little treat.

These were good days.

27

The next day was NOT a good day.

Something was very wrong. The crew members were having trouble with the car, and they could not figure out why. Race day was tomorrow, and they were running out of time.

The driver kept saying the car felt *off.* It sometimes *skipped a beat.* It wasn't *catching* sometimes. Revver learned that all this really meant that the car wasn't going as fast as they wanted it to go. When they tested the car on the track, everyone knew there was a problem, and Grumpy Jack was even grumpier than usual. Actually, *everyone* was grumpy. Revver remembered how he felt when the car he had made would not go and he could not figure out why. He guessed that everyone felt a lot like that. He felt sorry for all of them. He even felt a little sorry for Grumpy Jack.

Today, no one was very nice to Revver. When Revver tried to get close, the team kept shooing him away. "NOT NOW, Revver," they scolded. "Go hang out over there. Go on! We're too busy to mess around today." Everyone had their faces in and around the car, checking and tightening. They took things out and put them back in. But nothing seemed to fix the problem. The day wore on. The crew got grouchier and grouchier.

Even Bill was not very nice. He gave Revver food and water in a corner, but that was all. When Revver accidentally got in Bill's way, Bill yelled, **"Out of the way, Revver! We're busy! Stop getting underfoot!"** The yell made Revver jump. He felt a heavy knot in his stomach. Bill had never yelled at him before. In fact, he had never heard Bill yell at all before that. Back home, Sprite had scolded Revver often—so often that Revver was pretty used to it, and pretty good at ignoring it. But Bill's scolding felt different . . . and so much worse.

The air in the garage felt heavy. The crew worked late into the night, but they could not seem to fix the problem. No one laughed or whistled. No one even talked very much. They just said quick, gruff words in deep voices. The day felt long and dark.

Finally, Revver tucked himself into a pile of shop towels in the corner. Bill did not notice he was there or bother to fluff them, so Revver did his best to make them comfortable.

He felt very badly for the team. He felt very sorry for himself.

After a long time, Revver fell into a sad sleep.

28

He was sound asleep when he heard it: "Revver! Come quick! I need you!" Revver jolted awake and sat up, his eyes wide. *What was that? WHO was that?* He listened hard, but he didn't hear it again. He looked around the garage, but it was dark and empty; the team had finally gone to bed. He didn't hear anything except some crickets far, far away. After a while, he whispered, "Just a bad dream, I guess," and he settled in again.

He fell back to sleep. "Revver! Help!" He bolted to his feet and listened again. Nothing. Silence. But this time, he remembered the voice. It was Sprite's.

What a terrible dream! he thought. For sure, it

was even MORE terrible because this was the first time that he'd had a bad dream without Sprite to comfort him and talk to him when he woke up. He remembered the bad day. He remembered the bad dream. He remembered Sprite. Now he *really* missed her.

He couldn't tell if it was nighttime or very early in the morning, but there was no point in trying to sleep now. He was wide-awake.

He looked around the garage in the dim light. There was so much that he hadn't noticed with all the action of the crew running around. He saw tall rolling carts and giant toolboxes containing all sorts of magical, shiny-looking things. He saw power tools, floor jacks . . . and, of course, the car.

The more he noticed, the more excited he got!

Slowly and carefully at first, he started opening doors and drawers. He felt nervous and excited. He carefully touched things. He gently held every interesting item he could find, pretending he knew how to use it, making sound effects as he went along.

He poked in corners and peeked into bins. He climbed up onto benches and ladders to get a better look. Soon, he'd forgotten all about the bad dream. He also forgot all about being careful.

Now he wasn't nervous at all. This was fun! He felt happier.

There was a door he'd never noticed in the corner, so he pushed it open and went in. In the low light, he could see that, inside, there were many other doors. And there was just the right amount of space for a squirrel to easily crawl underneath!

He went under one of the doors and found himself in a little room. Most of the room was filled with a shiny white machine—some kind of engine maybe? It looked impressive! It must be very important to be in a room all by itself!

He jumped onto the round part and looked inside the machine and saw a pool of water. *Strange*, he thought, *that's the fuel?* It had no wheels. *How does it work? What does it do? Does this go INTO a car somehow?*

The machine was cold. Obviously it hadn't been running in a while. *How do they start it?* Revver walked all around the machine to inspect, and then he noticed a shiny metal lever near the top.

He jumped on top of the machine and tried moving the lever with his foot, but he couldn't budge it. He dropped back to the floor and tried pulling on it. He was able to move it a little, and it made a small gurgling sound, like the engine was trying to fire up. He tried harder. He jumped and grabbed the lever and hung from it, and the machine made the LOUDEST, most impressive roar as it started! Revver watched with excitement. As he hung from the lever, he noticed the water moving into a circle and then disappearing deep into a hole at the bottom. *Where did it go?* Before he had a chance to wonder, the water came back! He let go of the lever. He tried it again. Again, the water circled, disappeared, and returned. He did it again. And again. And again! He tried hanging off the lever longer to see what would happen. And again. And longer. And longer. Finally, he just hung on the lever as long as he could, watching the water swirling around and around.

But then, the water didn't disappear. Instead, it got higher and higher and began spilling out of the machine and onto the floor. Revver tried to stop it, but the lever wouldn't budge. It was stuck. The floor got wetter and wetter. Somehow, Revver knew something was wrong. He decided it was time to leave the machine alone.

He hurried out of the little machine room and shimmied back through the crack in the big door. He pushed against the door to make sure it was closed and went back into the main garage. He continued exploring, and, when he noticed it sitting there, alone, his heart skipped a beat.

There, in the darkness, just waiting for him, sat THE CAR.

29

He never got tired of seeing it. Even sitting still, it *looked* fast! It was so beautiful. So glorious. So **unsupervised**!

Just as he had that first day at the track, he jumped onto the hood, onto the roof, and rolled into the driver's seat. This time, he was careful not to get his foot tangled in the window net!

He picked up the pieces of the driver's special seat belt, the "five-point harness." It was a fascinating system: all the straps and connections that kept the driver safe. Revver remembered his ride in the car, being stuck against the back and then falling on his nose. He wondered if anyone could make a five-point harness for a squirrel.

He inspected every inch of the car. He touched and turned and wiggled absolutely everything. He went to the back, behind the driver's seat, behind the metal can, which he now knew was called the "fire bottle." He pretended the car was speeding around the track, just like that first day.

He kept exploring the inside of the car. He prodded and poked. He sat on the wheel well on the driver's side and slid down, like a little slide. He did it again. Then again. That time, **OUCH!** He felt a zap! He was confused. *I must have sat on a bee!* He looked for the bee while he rubbed the stingy feeling out of his bottom but didn't see one. He shrugged. *I guess it flew away*, he thought.

Then Revver went back up to the front seat of the car. He flipped a switch. He pushed a button. He flipped and pushed and pressed more things. *R-rrrrrrrrrrrr!* Something made the car roar to life! It surprised him, but it was AMAZING! The sound echoed through the garage. *Oh, it's magical!* he decided. He jumped down to the gas pedal on the floor, and the engine roared louder. *I just love that sound!*

He was dying to make it move! He wanted so badly to go *fast* again! But he knew he wasn't big enough to work the *shifter* by the seat with the *clutch* and the *pedals* on the floor. Bill had explained it to him: the driver had to work all of it together to make it go. Maybe tomorrow, Revver could try asking Bill to let him ride in the back, like he had that first day. Hopefully, Bill would be in a better mood tomorrow.

With the engine still racing, Revver jumped out the window opening.

There, in a corner, was what the team called a "creeper"—a little sled with wheels that some of the crew used to work under the cars. This gave Revver an AWESOME idea! He pushed it forward as he ran along behind, and then he jumped on. It rolled a few feet. "*Vrooooom!*" said Revver, imagining that he was driving a race car, moving ahead in the final turn.

I want to go faster! Revver decided to try a longer run. He pushed the creeper with his front paws and ran farther and faster before he jumped on. This time, he was able to get up some *real* speed! "*Woo-hoo!*" he squealed, imagining crossing the finish line to a checkered flag. Revver looked around for an even better, longer runway. He pushed some things out of the way until he had the perfect, clear space for a long, LONG run. He started up again: *push-run, push-run, push-run, JUMP ON!* He glided on the creeper, loving the feeling of air blowing through his whiskers!

Uh-oh! Revver bailed off just before the creeper hit the concrete wall ahead of him. The momentum threw him backward, and Revver went flying through the air, end over end over end—right into a tall rolling cart full of tools.

Bash!
Clankety!
Clang!
Clash!
Kaboom!

Revver, the cart, and the tools all crashed to the ground.

Revver heard a click, and a light went on. He heard someone yell, **"WHAT IN THE . . . ?"**

And there, with bulging eyes and a dark-red face, stood Grumpy Jack! Now he did not just look grumpy—he looked **MAD.**

Uh-oh, Revver thought. Jack's eyes met Revver's for a split second. Revver saw the veins on Jack's forehead, vibrating like branches in the wind. Jack made a grab for Revver's neck. Revver ducked just in time.

The white machine had continued leaking, and now the water started oozing under the door and into the main garage, soaking the shiny floor. Revver started running, feeling the cold water on his paws. Jack ran after him. More lights flicked on. All around him, Revver could see that crew members were running in, yelling as they stumbled over tools.

Jack almost caught Revver again, but Revver zigzagged. This time, Jack slipped and fell on the wet floor. Jack yelled again, and it was the loudest yell Revver had ever heard anything make, almost as loud as his own. Revver wanted to turn to look, but he didn't dare. Revver heard Jack get up and start the chase again. Revver kept running, zig-zagging every which way and climbing and jumping where he could, just like Mama had taught him.

Then Revver thought about Bill. Where was Bill? Bill could help him! Revver lost focus for a fraction of a second while he considered this, and then *Revver couldn't breathe*! Jack had caught him! He gripped Revver TIGHT around the neck, squeezing hard.

Jack was screaming at Revver. The car was roaring. The crew was yelling. Tools and equipment clanked and bashed. Revver caught the quickest sight of Bill, looking confused—and maybe even a little scared. Their eyes met just as Jack took Revver to the door, threw him into the air, and kicked him HARD across

the rear with a
steel-toe boot. Now
Revver's yelping added
to the chaos.

Revver landed, rolled, and
came to a stop a long way from the garage. It was
dark outside, except for a little bit of moonlight. He
rubbed his bottom, which was now sore from the
zap! AND the kick.

Revver sat, trying to sort his thoughts, when a
horrible, familiar smell caught his attention. Revver looked up. There, standing right in front of
him, was Farty.

"Revver, you have to come with us RIGHT
NOW. **Lick!**"

"He means 'quick.'"

"I mean **lick-spit!**"

"He means 'lickety-split.'"

Bounce had appeared. Revver was still trying
to collect himself and make sense of the last few
minutes. "But h-how d-did you know where to
find me?"

"It was easy."

"Mama helped us."

"B-but how did *she* know where I'd be?"

"Mama said, 'Just listen for trouble, and you'll find Revver.'"

"And here you are."

30

Bounce and Farty led the way. As they ran, the brothers told Revver what they knew. "Sprite fell," they said, panting out the details.

". . . a hole . . ."

"It's deep . . ."

"There's water . . ."

". . . And we can't get to her."

"We heard her calling for help."

"Mama said we need all the help we can get . . ."

"There are coyotes . . ."

The idea of coyotes made Revver shudder.

Revver thought about the dream that had woken him up. He remembered dreaming that

Sprite was calling for help. Could it have been real? How could he have heard her from so far away? How would that be possible?

Soon, they saw Mama standing at the base of a huge tree. They were much closer to the track than to their home tree. She was wringing her paws. Her eyes were red and her face was damp. Revver could tell that she had been crying.

"Why was Sprite over *here*?" Revver whispered, noticing how far they were from her walnut tree.

"She's been checking up on you."

"She has?"

"Mama told us to keep an eye on one another," Bounce said as Mama nodded. Revver had been so caught up with his own adventures he hadn't considered that. When he thought about Sprite, his heart hurt.

"Are the coyotes still there?" Bounce asked Mama.

Mama just nodded.

Quietly and carefully, Mama and the boys led

Revver a few trees away, and, without making a sound, they climbed up to look. They could see two coyotes below looking down into a deep hole with a metal grate on top. Revver could see how little Sprite could have easily fallen in the holes in the grate. She was so tiny. Mama, Bounce, and Farty whispered, "They were chasing her."

Mama sniffled. "She wasn't watching. She fell in while she was running away."

"I don't even think she could get out if they left. It's so steep and slippery in there."

"But they won't leave."

Revver thought about Sprite being chased and almost being eaten. He thought about her falling through the metal grate and into the deep hole. He thought about all the times she had been there for him, all the times she had saved him. This had happened because she was checking on him—because she cared about him. His thoughts were spinning. But Revver said nothing.

He didn't know what to do. He took a deep

breath and sat down to think. *Wait!* he thought. **Stop and think!** *That's right! That's one of my lessons!* He quickly sorted through all the other notes in his brain burrow for help. He needed ideas!

Revver looked through his notes carefully:

Revving is good SOMETIMES. He needed to give this some serious thought. *If revving is going to help, I have to be careful with it. I have to use it wisely,* he decided.

Everything is connected to everything else. He thought about the dream and how he had heard Sprite's voice. He thought about the team. He thought about his family. He thought about his work at the garage and all that he had learned. NOW he needed to take all that and help Sprite. This idea started to feel important.

No pooping in the garage. *Ugh! That won't help now!* He threw that note aside.

Learn from mistakes. Revver thought about this one a long time. He remembered all the times he'd done things without thinking and all the trouble it had caused. *I need to be careful. I need to be smart. Sprite's life depends on it.*

Little pictures of the past few days sparked through his brain like lightning bolts. Falling out of the tree. The hawk. The wall. Sprite. Working with the crew. The teamwork. The garage. The team owner. Wires and engines and hoists and tools . . .

Suddenly, energy ran through him. It was very un-Revver-like to plan, **BUT Revver had a plan!** He thought through the details one more time to be sure. *It could work. It has to,* he decided.

"We need to be a team," Revver said. "We can only win if we work like a team." He heard something in his own voice that was new. He sounded a little like Sprite when she used her serious "big sister" voice with him. He even sounded a little like Grumpy Jack when he barked orders at the team. It surprised him to hear himself.

Revver went on. "Everyone has an important part to play, and everyone has to do their job exactly right."

He had so much sureness in his voice that his mother and brothers didn't even question him.

"First, vines," Revver said. "We need vines. The strongest ones you can find: wild grapevines or bittersweet or creeping Charlie. We need to gather up as many as we can and bring them up top. *Quietly.* Don't let the coyotes hear or see you. *And hurry!*"

The three boys and Mama set about gathering vines and carrying them up to the treetop. Revver began winding, braiding, and weaving the vines to one another, making them into chains, exactly like he had seen Sprite do. He worked until the vines looked strong and thick like the chains in the garage. He twisted them together the way he'd seen Susan twist wires. He kept checking the pile of vines and kept looking at the distance down and into the hole. Again and again, he checked while he braided, twisted, and tied, trying to make sure he had enough.

"Now, while I'm doing this, fetch nuts. The biggest ones you can find. Farty, FETCHING, not eating." Farty nodded with his cheeks full of food.

"Bounce, wait. First, I need a rock, flat and very sharp. Can you find one?"

"On it."

In the meantime, Revver looked. He looked down at the drooling coyotes who were staring into the hole where Sprite was trapped. He looked around at the tree. He remembered what he'd learned from his *almost cannonball* into the nest. He remembered what he learned from all the midair grabs of the lug nuts—it was all about space and timing. He looked hard at the distance, and he finally decided that he needed the coyotes just a little closer to the tree. He adjusted the plan again. Then he thought through everything one last time. With everyone listening, Revver told them exactly what needed to happen.

Grumpy Jack popped into Revver's head, and Revver understood what the team owner must feel: it was important that everyone do their job exactly right. It was the only way it would all work. In racing, it was the only way they could win. Here, it was the only way to save Sprite.

The plan was set. They were ready to go.

31

"Back away RIGHT NOW, or you'll regret it!" Mama stood at the base of the tree. The coyotes looked up from the hole, surprised. They laughed at Mama and did not move.

"I *said*, BACK AWAY FROM THERE—OR YOU'LL BE SORRY!" she said again, louder.

Instead of backing away, the two coyotes raised up and inched toward Mama, licking their chops and drooling. From his spot on the branch, Revver could see that they were now in the perfect position.

"Vr-vr-vr-VRRROOOOM!" Revver screamed. The coyotes stopped walking toward Mama and looked up, confused by the sound.

"Farty, jump!" Revver ordered. Farty leapt HARD on a giant, thick limb, just away from the V place that the squirrels had cut loose by scratching and cutting with the sharp rock.

Revver roared again, keeping the coyotes' attention so they didn't move away. **"Vr-vr-vr-VRRROOOOM!"**

Now even more confused, they sat back to look—and Farty jumped once more and then jumped back just in time. The giant limb fell and crashed, right on top of the coyotes!

The two coyotes fell flat and whimpered in pain.

A thought struck Revver as quickly as the branch struck the coyotes. Just like Mama had warned them, those coyotes WERE sorry! Mama was always true to her word. Then a thought made him shiver: *Mama does not bluff.* He forced himself to shake off the what-ifs of that idea and get back to work.

The coyotes were hurt. But they stumbled back

to their place on top of the grate. The squirrels still could not get to Sprite, and Sprite had no way to get out.

"Now!" Revver commanded. Aiming for the coyotes' faces, all four squirrels began pummeling the coyotes with nuts, throwing them as hard as they could. They all aimed well, but Revver's aim was *perfect*. All that practice with the lug nuts had paid off.

Revver gave a final warning, with his loudest **"Vr-vr-vr-VRRROOOOM!"** and the defeated coyotes pulled themselves up and limped far away—as quickly as they could stumble.

"Part two!" Revver shouted.

Sprite could fit through the holes in the grate, but none of the others could. They needed to move that heavy iron lid to help her.

The four squirrels got right to work. Revver ran down to the base of the tree and tied one end of the braided vines through the holes in the iron grate and knotted it. He studied the knot. It looked like the chain on the hoist that held the engine. He hoped he had done it right. He hoped it would hold.

"Sprite, we're coming!" he yelled into the hole. He heard nothing back. This scared him, but he forced himself to focus on the plan.

The other end of the vine went up into the tree, hung over a high branch, and then dangled back to the ground, just like the engine hoist in the garage. Revver had made a pulley system to help them lift the heavy grate.

Now on the ground, all four squirrels pulled as hard as they could. Nothing budged.

Revver remembered how he was finally able to start up the white machine in the garage. "Farty, go up higher, then jump and hang on the vine," he ordered.

Farty jumped and hung, and the grate lifted. "Stay there! Hold on!" Revver yelled. He ran over to the hole and guided the grate away from the hole, remembering how the crew had guided the engine into the car from the hoist. "Perfect," he said. "Lower it down *very slowly*." Revver continued to guide the grate away from the hole, leaving a Bounce-sized gap. Farty scooted off the vine, back onto the ground with the rest of them.

"Bounce, are you ready?" Revver asked. Bounce stood at attention on his back paws with his arms out wide, not moving a muscle. Revver twisted vines around him, tight and secure, trying to remember exactly how the five-point harness worked. Finally, it looked right. "It makes sense for *you* to go," Revver told him. "Farty is too heavy, and I need his help on the ground. Plus, you have the strongest arms and legs. Are you sure you're ready?"

Only then did Bounce start bouncing. He was ready.

Bounce dangled from the end of a vine, and Mama, Farty, and Revver held the other end, lowering Bounce slowly into the hole. Bounce disappeared into the dark well. The other three kept

slowly feeding vine—more, and more, and more, taking Bounce lower and lower into the black hole.

Revver looked back and watched the pile of braided vine disappear. He panicked. They were running out! Maybe he hadn't tied enough?! Now there were only a few yards left . . . then one yard . . . then a foot . . . then a few inches. Revver tried to remain calm and think. He felt sure he had estimated correctly! Sprite had been down there for so long already; he couldn't stand the idea of having to start over. And what if the coyotes came back?!

"Got her!" Bounce's voice finally echoed in the hole. Revver and Mama sighed with relief, and Farty let out a looong, serious stinker that was so alarming Revver's grip almost slipped off the vine.

"Hold her tight," Mama pleaded to Bounce as

Mama, Farty, and Revver all began to pull up on the vine. They pulled with every ounce of strength they had. Their arms were already tired from lifting the metal grate and lowering Bounce. And pulling up was SO MUCH harder than lowering down. Plus, now they were lifting Bounce's AND Sprite's weight. But they kept pulling, inch by inch, slowly, s-l-o-w-l-y . . . until, finally, Bounce and Sprite lifted out of the hole. Revver jumped over and gently pulled Bounce's tail to guide Bounce and Sprite away from the hole. The others lowered them safely onto the grass. Revver looped the rope around the tree and made a tight knot. He removed Bounce's harness.

As the whole rescue unfolded, Mama kept watching Revver. Somehow, he had learned the Essential Squirrel Skills after all. But it was clear that living at the track had taught him so much more. Somehow—all the things that he *had* learned—connected to everything else.

32

Sprite looked awful. She was weak, shivering—and filthy. Her fur was flattened because she was soaking wet, so she looked even tinier than usual. Revver would not have recognized her.

Everyone spent the rest of the night taking care of her: fetching small bites of food, filling nut-shells with water for Sprite to sip, and wrapping her in large leaves for warmth. Revver mostly stayed back to keep Sprite warm and keep her company.

Revver and Sprite chatted quietly about all that had happened the last few days. Sprite had been happy and enjoying life in the walnut tree, but she always made a point of checking on

Revver. The coyotes had surprised her when she was on her way to the track earlier. Mama had gotten worried when Sprite didn't return to her new home in the walnut tree. When Mama discovered what had happened, she'd gathered Revver's brothers for help, and they found Revver.

Revver told Sprite his stories about the garage and the team owner and all the trouble that had happened before he'd come back. "Oh, BROTHER! You *DIDN'T!*" she squealed and laughed weakly when Revver told her about the accident with the creeper. "Oh *NOOO!*" she gasped when Revver told her about being ACTUALLY kicked out of the garage by the team owner. They both giggled when Revver showed her his bruised tail to prove it. Sprite noticed the sparkle in Revver's eyes when he talked about the car and helping the crew and watching the practice runs and the pit stops—and especially when he spoke about Bill.

They talked and talked. After some time, Sprite seemed to get back to her old self.

Once Mama was sure that all was well, she

hugged the others and headed back to the old tree. "Do try to be careful, dears," she said. "I'm getting too old for all this action." Then she hugged Revver. "I'm proud of you," she whispered in his ear. It was the first time that Mama had ever said that. As Mama said her goodbyes, Revver and Sprite both noticed something: Mama was wearing a braided chain around her neck—a very fancy design with a little acorn attached to it. Sprite clutched Revver's paw, and they smiled at each other.

Bounce, practically bouncing out of his paws, was eager to run off as well. But he felt dutiful and wanted to be polite. "How much longer should I stay?" he asked. "I mean, I *can* stay. I will stay." *Boing-boing!* He bounced with each word. "Should I stay?" *Boing!* "Sprite, do you need me to stay? I mean, I *will* . . ." *Boing-boing-boing!*

Sprite looked at Bounce, bouncing. "Oh, *brother*," Sprite said. "I'm fine now, Bounce. Thank you for, you know, everything. I'm so grateful. I'll see you around the tr—"

She had not even gotten the last word out

before Bounce had disappeared into the darkness in a brown flash. Revver, Farty, and Sprite all laughed as they watched him take off.

After a bit of silence, Farty looked at Revver and Sprite. "I *am* getting a little bit hungry," he said hopefully.

"Go *ahead*," Revver and Sprite said together. Sprite stood and hugged Farty hard. "Thank you so much, sweet, sweet brother," she whispered. *Pffft!* She had accidentally pushed a bit of air out of him, and she held her breath. Farty hugged her back for a moment and then walked away, sniffing the ground for treats as he went.

"Oh, *brothers*," Sprite whispered, nothing but thankful for them.

"I'll walk you back to your tree," Revver said once Farty was out of sight.

It had been a big night, and a long one. Revver had not slept since the dream about Sprite woke him up. Once they arrived at Sprite's walnut tree, they cozied into a deep burrow—and fell sound asleep.

33

Even before he was completely awake, Revver started sniffing the air. He began to feel tingly and jittery. It was still dark. The sun was just barely peeking up, but he could just SENSE it. He knew: it was **race day.**

Sprite was still sleeping when Revver climbed to the top of the tree, hoping that he might be able to see something at the track. The view was not as good from here as from their old tree. He could see a few lights, but not much else. Nothing else, in fact.

He sighed and went back down to sit with Sprite.

She was awake. "You're still here?" she asked.

"Of course I'm still here. Where else would I be?"

"What do you mean *where else?* The track, of course."

"I can't go back there."

"Don't be silly. Why not?"

"Well, I can't leave you, for one. And two, I don't have any place there."

"Revver, of course you can leave me. I'm fine! And you DO have a place there—with Bill and the team. It's what you always wanted."

"You need me."

Sprite let out a big laugh. "Not!" she said.

"Oh, *right*. What about yesterday?"

Sprite rolled her eyes. "Okay. Well, I'm pretty sure THAT won't happen again."

"Sprite, I'm serious."

"Little brother, I will be just fine. I promise you."

For some reason, *little brother* didn't bother him this time.

"Am I right?"

"I guess," he admitted. He knew his sister. He

somehow just *knew* she *would* be okay. He knew Sprite better than anyone. She was a lot stronger than she looked.

"Plus, you HAVE to go. It's your dream. You can't give up your dream. You just can't."

"It's not *really* my dream."

"Stop it, Revver. I SAW you. After you went for the ride in the car. And at the track, with the human—Bill."

"You SAW me?"

"Of course."

Silence.

"But you know what I *really* saw, Revver? I saw you HAPPY. I saw you the kind of happy that I feel when I'm making things or playing on my swings. Or how Farty feels when he has a delicious meal or Bounce feels when he's jumping around. I saw you HAPPY. And you know what else?"

"What else?"

"When I saw you there, Revver, I *understood*."

Revver felt his heart jump a beat. "I messed everything up."

"Yep, you made a HUGE mess!" She laughed.

"It's not funny."

"Revver, you can't give up just because it's hard or because you made a mistake."

Revver heard Bill's voice in his memory: *learn from mistakes, learn from mistakes, learn from mistakes* . . . But how would the team ever want him back? He'd made *such* a mess of things. At last, Revver sighed. "I don't know."

"Sometimes things are just hard, but you can't give up. You have to be brave."

"Sprite," Revver whispered, "I really, *really* messed up."

Sprite thought for a few seconds. "Well, at least you could go back over to watch the race today, right?"

"How did you know there's a race?"

Sprite sighed. "Oh, *brother*. Because I know you."

34

Revver slowly started to make his way back to the track, toward the infield, toward the garage. With every step, *ouch!* His butt really hurt! He rubbed it, remembering Jack's boot kick. He remembered the *zap!* of the bee sting that had come *before* the boot kick.

Wait. Revver stopped cold.

WAIT. WAIT. WAIT! The zap! The zap! **THE ZAP!** Revver's mind started racing. He started to run. He ran faster and faster. If Bounce had been running with him, Revver would have left him miles behind. Revver had never run faster, EVER. He was panicking . . . How would he get in? Would they even let him near the car? How would he get them to understand? Would he be on time? What if Jack saw him?

All the pieces started to come together: Mama's warning about power lines . . . the car's wiring . . . the *zap* . . . ! Revver had felt it when he was sliding down the wheel well, right on top of where the battery sat and the wiring started. There was no bee sting! He had felt **electricity**! There was a short in the wiring! One of the wires either had a break or wasn't connected just right. Maybe Revver had made a mistake when he installed it, or it could be the wire was just damaged. It didn't matter in any case. What mattered was that Revver now knew— he KNEW!—THAT was the problem with the car!

Revver was small . . . He could get in there without anyone having to take anything apart! He could work fast. There was still time, and he knew what to do! He could fix it!

As he ran and ran, words and thoughts ran with him . . . All the way, he whispered to himself what Sprite had just told him. "Be brave. Be brave. Be brave."

35

It was still barely light outside when Revver got to the garage. He peeked in. His mess had been cleaned up and all the tools were back in their place.

Susan and a few other crew members were looking over the car, exactly the way they had looked when Revver fell asleep last night. So much had happened since then!

Susan scratched her head. Still, no one looked happy. Revver could tell that they had not slept much.

Revver went in. No one noticed him.

Revver rushed over to Susan, who was bent over the engine. He tugged on Susan's pant leg, but she didn't pay attention. Revver tugged again, but she was too busy to notice.

Revver planted his feet and took a breath. **"Vr-ur-ur-VRRROOOOM!"** Someone dropped a wrench and it clanged to the floor. Everyone stood looking at Revver. Someone said, "Get him out of here. If Jack sees him in here, he'll have a fit." Susan picked Revver up by the scruff and started toward the door.

"No!" Revver yelled. "No! You don't understand! Stop! Stop! I can help! I can fix it!" Revver wiggled and twisted to try to get free. Desperate, he reached up and gave Susan a good scratch on the hand.

"Ouch! Darn it!" she yelled as she dropped Revver. "Bill! Help me with your squirrel! I don't have time to mess around this morning!"

Now Revver panicked.

Revver darted back to the car. Susan and Bill gave chase, but Revver was too quick. He ran under the car and jumped into the wheel well near the battery. Bill flattened himself onto his stomach and tried reaching for Revver, but the space was too tight. All Bill could do was strain to see. "Dude, whatcha doin'? Come outta there now, Revver. We gotta get out to the track this morning. There's no time for playing." Bill didn't sound angry, but he sounded very tired.

Revver poked his head out to look at Bill for a second. Their eyes met again. Revver knew that he had no time to waste. He jumped back into the wheel well.

Revver closed his eyes so he could concentrate. Bill kept talking to him, asking him to come out, but Revver could not pay attention. He had to focus. He had to **stop and think.**

Revver carefully and slowly felt the length of the wire with his paw. Nothing. *Concentrate!* he told himself. He ran his paw along the wire again. Still nothing. Again, he ran his paw along the wire. *There!* He felt it this time . . . the tiniest *zap!* He had found where the wire was broken! *Now, how do I fix it?* There was no time to run a whole new piece.

Revver tugged the wire. There was *just enough* slack that Revver could cut away the broken part and twist the wires back together. But he had to do it perfectly or the vibration of the car would make it come loose during the race. *I can do this,* he thought. Revver was an expert at twisting and braiding now!

Revver was so deep in thought that he did not notice that half the crew was on the floor watching him now. They were straining to see what he was doing under the car. Everyone watched. There were a few whispers, a few very quiet *oohs* and *aahs*. Revver did not hear them.

Revver unhooked the wire from the battery to stop the electricity. He bit away JUST the small piece that was broken. He twisted the wire back together. *It has to be perfect,* he knew. And it *was* perfect—even Sprite would have been impressed by his work. He reconnected the top of the wire to the battery. He checked his work. **Everything is connected to everything else.** At last, he was sure.

There! It's done.

Revver came out from under the car. He did what he had to do. Now he prepared himself. He waited for someone to scream at him or grab him by the scruff or kick him out the door.

Instead, the whole crew started clapping.

36

There was no doubt that Revver was going to watch the race. Bill and the others hid him in the pit box, behind some tools. Revver felt the jostling as the pit box was moved from the garage and set in place on pit road. When the moving stopped, Revver remained very still until it felt safe. Finally, he poked his head out for a quick peek. *Jack's not looking this way!* Revver jumped out.

Race day! From pit road! He was more nervous and excited than he'd ever felt in his life. All the work and practicing and testing that he'd seen the crew doing—that he'd helped with—came down to this day, to this race. But he was still scared. *What if Jack sees me? What then?*

Jack was watching the race from the top of the pit wagon. He wore headphones and held binoculars. Revver needed to be very, very careful.

Revver put his paw over his heart when he heard the national anthem, just like he'd seen a million times from the tree. He felt very earnest. Then he heard the grand marshal yell, *"Drivers, start your engines!"* and he saw the pace car and felt the vibration of all the cars behind it, and he knew that this was the moment they had all been awaiting.

Revver stood, hidden but focused. Watching the race from pit road was *so awesome!* It was all so close! It was all so beautifully **FAST**. Even though Revver was worried about Jack spotting him, it was better than he had ever imagined.

Their car was running GREAT! The driver had worked his way up to the lead! Every once in a while, someone on the team would catch Revver's eye and give him a "thumbs-up"!

After a while, their driver pulled onto pit road. When the car was one pit stall away, the entire crew: the fuel guy, the jackman, the tire carrier, Bill, and the other tire changer all jumped over the wall and into action. It was an incredible thing to watch. Revver felt a great sense of pride that he had played a part in all this.

As soon as the car stopped, the fuel guy started filling the car, the jackman lifted the right side of the car, and Bill jumped to the rear tire and squatted down. *Zhhht-zhhht-zhhht-zhhht-zhhht!* Five lug nuts dropped to the ground. The tire changer took the old tire away, put the new tire on, and Bill zipped his impact wrench around to secure it: *zhhht-zhhht-zhhht-zhhht-zhhht!*

The other tires were changed the same way while the gas man topped off the fuel and someone else used a brush on a long stick to clean off the front grill. The jack dropped the left side of the car to the ground, signaling that the pit stop was complete. The car squealed away, leaving its pit stall behind as it headed down pit road and back onto the track.

The car rolled over the lug nuts on the asphalt

and shot them in all directions like tiny rockets. Remembering how he'd gathered them for Bill inside the garage, Revver couldn't help but watch them fly. One in particular glimmered in the sunlight and caught his eye. It flew to the right of the team, toward the pit behind them. In a bit of a trance, Revver kept watching as it hit the ground.

That's why Revver saw it happen when no one else on the team did. A few pit stalls behind them, a tire had somehow gotten away from the tire carrier and was rolling into the middle of pit road just as another car was squealing away from its pit stall. *Ka-thud!* The car collided with the runaway tire. The tire flew into the air, bounced, and went airborne again—heading straight for the top of the team's pit wagon—*and right toward Jack's head!*

There was no time at all to think, but all the lug-nut catching had given Revver exceptional aim. With all the power his furry legs could give him, Revver leapt toward the team owner. **"Vr-vr-vr-VRRROOOOOOOOOOOOOM!"** pierced through all the other noise around them.

Jack turned to look just in time to see the squirrel flying right toward his face. Revver could see Jack's mouth open wide in surprise. He could also see the angry look in Jack's eyes when Jack realized that it was Revver flying toward him.

Revver grabbed onto Jack's head. The two of them fell back just as the tire barely missed both of them, sailed over their heads, and landed safely on the ground behind them with a muffled **thud!**

Jack had not seen the tire, and he was fierce with anger. He threw Revver off as hard as he could. Revver somersaulted through the air. He flew, he flipped, and, finally, he rolled on the ground, back onto pit road. He landed, dizzy. Once he finally found his footing, his only instinct was to run—as fast as he could—away from Jack.

He leapt from the infield toward the outside wall between turns three and four, with the black #4 car just missing him. Revver snapped to realization: *"What am I doing?! I'm on the track! I'm on the TRACK—DURING THE RACE!"* He felt the wind from the right-side tire of the black car nearly catch his tail. *Now Revver was running for his life!*

Somewhere inside, a voice was telling him to get back to the safety of the infield, but he was still dizzy, and his vision was blurry from all the smoke. He couldn't sense which way to go! He felt the heat of an engine on his side and turned. This time, the yellow #2 car missed him by a whisker. He dodged left and was almost hit again. A split second later, a bumper almost smashed into him head-on, and he dodged it just in time.

The squirrel squealed for his life, but his scream was completely drowned out by the engines. He kept running, jumping, and spinning on the steamy asphalt, dodging car after car and burning-hot grills and tailpipes by only a hair.

Revver's entire short life flashed before his eyes. He saw himself as a baby squirrel, always fascinated with the track and the cars. His mother's and his siblings' chanting echoed through his ears like a nightmarish song that wouldn't stop:

"And what's the rule on cars?"

"If you get near that, you'll end up FLAT!"

Desperately, he began to plead, "PLEASE! Somebody throw a caution! Wave the yellow flag! I'm going to die! *I'M GOING TO DIE!!!*"

But no one slowed down. The track was hot and sticky, and he struggled to move his paws on the gluey surface. He was moving in slow motion, but the cars were going faster and faster. The whole world was a blur.

Suddenly, ahead of him, Revver saw a wall. He wasn't sure if it was the infield wall or the outside wall because he was so turned around, but it was his last hope. He took a deep breath, screamed for all he was worth, and leapt off the sticky asphalt with every ounce of strength he had.

Everything went black.

37

Revver was on his back, looking up at the sky. The sun was shining behind a large person, who looked down at him. The person's face was in shadow. All Revver could see were the bright sun-rays all around them. *Oh no*, he thought, *I must be dead*. He squinted and tried to focus.

The figure spoke back. "You're awake! Hey, little dude, that was quite a show you put on earlier! That was some fast, fancy action back there, that's *ferrrr sure*! I gotta tell ya, though, none of us were certain you made it through. Sure took me a while to find you here, little buddy!"

Revver looked up, still confused. It took him a moment to realize he *wasn't* dead. He was lying on a patch of grass in the infield, and it was Bill talking to him.

The squirrel's head felt heavy. He felt like he couldn't breathe, that he was choking. In panic, he sat up, inhaled, and coughed hard . . .

And out popped— One. Yellow. Lug nut.

Bill jumped back in surprise. "Whoa! Dude! I told you before! You have GOT to stop trying to eat those!" Bill started laughing and shaking his head.

Revver sighed, exhausted, and let his head drop back on the ground.

Bill looked into Revver's dull black eyes and saw his little mouth and whiskers pointing down, and Bill knew exactly what Revver was thinking. Bill's own heart nearly broke when he realized it.

"Hey, buddy, you're a hero!" Bill continued. "No one's mad atcha, not even Jack! You saved ol' Jack's life back there! And you'll never believe it:

we won today! Revver! You helped us win!!! Jack's come to thinking that you're some kind of good luck charm for us! Dude, we're sure not gettin' rid of ya anytime soon! You wanna come back to the team, right?"

The sadness started to leave Revver's face.

"Hey, buddy, it's all fine! You got a little carried away in the garage, that's all. I understand."

I understand. Those words echoed around in Revver's head, over and over. For Revver's whole life, he'd longed for someone to *understand.* Now he had Sprite's blessing. And he had Bill. Some things were even more important than being fast or winning.

Revver looked into Bill's face and blinked. A sparkle began to return to the squirrel's small black eyes.

"Tell you what, little Revver: we're getting packed up and ready to head out after a while. 'Another place, another race' next weekend, ya know. I'm pretty sure we can find room for you if you wanna come along with the team. You can rest up a bit. And when you're ready, you can get back to helping out in the garage. And ol' Jack thinks you should be our spotter from the pits on race days—you know, to keep an eye on things. After all, it wouldn't be right to leave one of our own behind after all you did for us."

Revver felt the big knot inside start to disappear.

"Oh, and hey," Bill went on. "Since it seems like you have a hankering for speed, I suppose we can sneak you a ride in the car once in a while—you know, so you stay out of trouble in the garage?" Bill winked.

Revver sat up.

"You sure are somethin', little Revver. So, whaddaya say? You wanna join the crew?"

Revver was excited by the idea! But then he thought harder. *I'd be leaving. I'd be going far, far away—from Mama and my brothers . . . and from Sprite.*

Revver put his head back on the ground and closed his eyes. He dug through his brain burrow to see if there was anything in there that could help him. Finally, he found it: Everything is connected to everything else.

He thought hard about this. He thought about how he'd loved racing and cars before he could remember anything else. He remembered the dream and hearing Sprite calling for help. He thought hard about his family. He thought about Sprite and how she knew he was happy. *We'll always be connected*, he thought. *I'm connected to racing, but I'm connected to my family, too. Being apart doesn't change anything.* Almost as if Sprite were standing right in front of him, Revver clearly heard her voice: *You HAVE to go. It's your dream. You can't give up your dream. Be brave.*

Revver jumped to his feet and began chattering. "I'd LOVE to be part of the team! No one in my family ever understood how much I love cars and racing and going *fast*—but you, YOU and the rest of the crew, you are like me. You *understand*." Revver went on. "So do you think the team might be able to get a matching fire suit to fit me? Does anyone make very tiny tools? And I was thinking that I could use a five-point harness, you know, for safety. Or maybe . . ." But Revver stopped when he saw Bill's expression, and remembered that Bill could not understand one word of Squirrel.

Revver steadied himself with both feet, clenched his fists, inhaled deeply, and said, **"Vr-vr-vr-VRRROOOOM!"**

Bill laughed. "Yep. You sure are somethin', little guy. I'm gonna assume that's a yes."

Revver nodded, better than any squirrel had ever nodded, ever: a very, VERY human nod.

Bill laughed again and picked Revver up from the ground. He placed Revver on his shoulder, and Revver held on tightly as they walked away. "So, buddy, I gotta ask you," Bill said. He kept walking as he looked up at Revver. "Was that you who broke the toilet and flooded the place?"

Revver hesitated. Then he gave one very SMALL nod, admitting what he'd done.

Bill shook his head and laughed. "Okay, bud, I'll tell you what. We'll keep that between us.

I convinced Jack that was just a coincidence. But you gotta promise me that won't happen again, okay? You made a heck of an awful mess. Toilets are not toys. Got it?"

Revver thought about the white machine with the water that he now knew had the name "toilet." He nodded. Then Revver wrote a note for his brain burrow, *Toilets are not toys*, and he filed the idea safely away.

They headed toward the infield garage to pack up and head out for the next track. Revver's adventures were just beginning.

In the surrounding trees, Revver's mother, brothers, and sister had watched it all through their own acorn binoculars.

"Brothers." Sprite sighed—sad to see Revver

leaving but mostly very happy. Sprite was, after all, a lot stronger than she looked.

Mama, Bounce, Farty, Sprite, and Revver were all smiling—as best as squirrels can smile. Finally, after a long while, the whole family went back to their very squirrelly activities . . . gathering nuts, bouncing, and swinging through the trees.

All except one.

Acknowledgments

I owe so much to so many people who helped make this, my first novel (SQUEE!!!), possible!

For William Campana, our personal NASCAR insider, my tech advisor, and a wonderful friend to our family—and to Revver. Bill, you are amazing, and I owe you a debt of gratitude.

For Chris Buescher, thank you for a front-row view from the pits and for welcoming us and "Little Zak" into your racing family. Zak still races #60 in honor of you and those amazing experiences. We're so proud to know you and thrilled for all of your success; we're cheering for you every race weekend. We wish you Godspeed and checkered flags, always.

For Cissa Barbosa, Nancy Mansfield, Stacy McAnulty, and all three Rinker boys—for reading and critiquing from the earliest (awful!) drafts. (And, Stacy, thank you for going to bat for me with Lori to help Farty keep his name.) Thanks also to Andie Detzel, Ben Michael, and Claire Lewandowski for last-minute read-throughs.

For Maya Myers, I'm grateful for your guidance and assistance.

Lori Kilkelly, my incredible agent, advocate, therapist, and friend: so many wonderful things have happened in my career because you led the way. Thank you for encouraging this project based on a pitch that, I'm sure, sounded crazy. Thank you for all the ways you "get" me. I'm beyond grateful for your support and encouragement. You're equally kind and tough as nails, and I'm thankful for both sides of you.

Alex Willan, thank you for illustrating this book; I could not be more thrilled.

For Mary Kate Castellani, my fabulous editor: you are a wonder. I'm so, SO blessed that you agreed to take on this rookie and this crazy idea and nurture Revver and his story through your ideas and insights. Delving into the life of this squirrel family came at a time I truly needed the diversion; your support and patience helped more than you can know.

With so many thanks to my amazing Bloomsbury team! Ksenia Winnicki, Faye Bi, Erica Barmash, Lily Yengle, Beth Eller, Jasmine Miranda, Allison Moore, Oona Patrick, Nick Sweeney, Melissa Kavonic, and everyone else who worked on this book.

For Nancy Rinker, my proofreader and cheerleader, thank you for being "Mom" to me.

For Zak Rinker, my brown-eyed boy: your wit, your love of speed, and your passion for anything with a motor has inspired me in a million ways.

For my oldest son, Ben, who, at the age of four, taught us one of life's most important truths: *everything is connected to everything else.*

And, for Faith.